# PURSUING REBECCA BEDFORD

## AUDREY LANE BLENHEIM

ISBN-13: 978-0-578-85828-9

# CONTENTS

*To Mom and Dad, who have been pointing me to Jesus through every turn of my life and will always be my biggest fans.*

"And we know that for those who love God all things work together for good, for those who are called according to his purpose."

— ROMANS 8:28

*H*er back was stiff, her jaw set at a stubborn angle, and her hands still. The whispering women had not yet discovered her presence. The ridiculously oversized flower arrangement in the center of the dining room served as the perfect hiding place.

"Can you imagine such a thing?" Anne giggled. "A young woman turning down such an advantageous offer of marriage? It reminded me of Rebecca and John Templeton two years ago. I do hope young Mary is not following in Rebecca's footsteps of poor decisions."

Harriett was quick to add in her tales. "Speaking of Rebecca Bedford, did you hear the latest? Rebecca has been selling her music compositions on the side to bring in her own money. Sheer desperation, if you ask me."

"At least it is music. She is not giving up her femininity completely. But surely she does not think men will find such willful independence attractive."

"Of course not! Men want someone who will be content to raise their children, run their home, and not seek ways to build independence. It's absurd for her to think she will ever receive another offer of marriage."

"She's mad. I've been saying it for years."

"Harriett! How you do run on! That's a cruel thing to say. I do not think she can help it. You know the rumors that her mother was insane."

"The poor dear. She may have overcome having such a mother had she stayed the course her father worked so hard to carve for her. She is dooming herself to be an old maid."

"Well, after that whole scandal with John Templeton, I think she was doomed long ago," Anne tsked. "Did you know that John spent three hours trying to convince her not to break off the engagement? She would have none of it."

"Three hours? I heard that he barely argued with her. He was completely humiliated in front of everyone. Why would he fight to keep her?"

"Well, he did. I have it straight from Tom. That's

when she threw his ring out the window and into the street!"

Both girls grew quiet for a moment. Rebecca wondered what had distracted them, then she heard her brother's voice.

"Hello, Miss Gosbee! Miss Whitlow!"

"Well, Henry Bedford, what a wonderful surprise. We were just talking about your sister. You know how I adore her."

Rebecca caught herself before a snort slipped out. Anne Whitlow had been shamelessly flirting with Henry since she was twelve years old. She was always daring to use his Christian name in public, throwing her arm through his, and laughing at everything he said as if he was the most entertaining person in every room. Their parents had been life-long friends, and they had spent many days together when they were young. Of course, just because parents were friendly did not mean their children were destined to be.

Graciously, Henry bowed his head toward them, and Rebecca smiled to herself. Henry was a better person, down to his very soul, than she could ever hope to be. He was a gentleman through and through, caring deeply for every living thing he met, regardless of social standing. He was not ignorant of social barriers, raised as astutely as Rebecca had been. But where Rebecca ignored barriers by creating scandal and uproar, Henry did so quietly, patiently, and gently. He never did anything worthy of a raised eyebrow, unless it was to receive praise of his caring heart.

"Miss Whitlow, it is wonderful to see you. I trust your family is well?"

"They are, thank you. I trust you heard our dear Albert is back in British Columbia?"

"I did. Please give him my congratulations on a job well done at Dalhousie."

"We will. Please, Henry, join us for tea."

"I will have to decline as I am here to meet Rebecca."

Anne fell momentarily silent, and when she recovered, there was a panicked hilt to her voice. "Oh. Is she here? I have not spotted her."

Henry poked his finger in her direction. "I believe I see her over there on the other side of that floral arrangement."

Rebecca sighed. She would now have to say hello. She rose from her chair and made her way toward the table.

"Good morning, Anne, Harriett," she dipped her head at them.

"Good morning, Rebecca," Harriett smiled, both

women's cheeks flushing red. "How long have you been here? We did not see you come in."

"I arrived long before you did, I believe," Rebecca told them. "You were so deep in conversation I could not bring myself to interrupt."

She fixed Anne with a pointed stare as she went on. "There does not seem to be much in the way of the society papers on this particular day. I would have to resort to discussing old matters. So please, don't let us keep you."

Rebecca backed away, knowing both ladies' averted eyes meant she had chastised them quite enough to sink further on the list of people they merely tolerated because society deemed it necessary. Somehow, she was sure she was more embarrassed than they were.

"Well, have a wonderful day, Henry," Anne spoke. "You as well, Rebecca."

Henry bowed his head toward them once more and then followed Rebecca to the table she had claimed for the two of them. They both assumed a chair, and Henry set his hat in his lap, offering her a warm brotherly smile.

"Well, sister," he greeted her. "Have you ordered?"

"Only tea," she told him. "I told the waiter to return when you arrived."

She set about pouring his cup of tea. The waiter

was two tables away, taking down an order, and she knew he would soon appear at their side. Her burning question would have to wait a moment longer.

"You missed Gran's visit last night," Rebecca told him. "Of course, she immediately forgave your absence."

"That visit happens weekly. I figure I can miss one or two."

"As the favorite grandchild, you have the fortune of missing whatever you like without it harming your reputation. You may as well be King Edward himself with the way Father goes on about your *many* achievements. I do not know that *I* will forgive your absence. You know how it turns all attention to my faults when you are not there to praise."

Henry winced. "Was it awful?"

The waiter appeared then, and they ordered their scones and fruit. When they were alone again, Rebecca answered him.

"Oh, I heard the usual critiques that I am hearing everywhere these days. Gran reminded me that no man wants to touch me with a twelve-foot pole. She is convinced I might have recovered from the scandal with John if I had not been so dramatic in my handling of it. She's not wrong. I acted foolishly.

I had never been so humiliated and injured, and I stopped thinking. I simply reacted."

A sigh fell from his lips. "The only fool in that room was John. I am sorry, Rebecca. I truly thought they would have let it go by now. John obviously had his way with Cynthia, even running off to London with her."

"Don't apologize. My social standing makes no impact on my happiness. I'm not as simple as some people. I can find happiness in things outside of homemaking and being a wife and mother."

"You cannot convince me that you will be content to be single your whole life," Henry argued. "I watched you, walking around with your dolls and wearing wedding clothes, imagining your future."

"Show me a little girl in our society that is not brought up to want that and that alone," she told him. "Yes, I dreamed of that at one point. But the reality of men has shocked that completely out of me."

"John is a fool," Henry told her. "But I assure you they are not all like him."

"You and you alone are the only truly good man on this earth, Henry," Rebecca told him, stirring her tea with her teaspoon. "You must keep your promise to only marry a woman as truly good as you, no matter what Papa arranges. You hold your ground,

Henry Bedford. For I'm sure, there isn't a financial gain in the world more important than the happiness of your heart."

He smiled, and she was sure she saw the hint of a secret in his eyes but she would wait to ask another day. Her mind could not help but wander to the tittering females across the room with their less than graceful opinion of her. Rebecca admitted to herself that she had fallen from grace, tumbling from her place in society as Paul Alexander Bedford's daughter and heiress. The engagement scandal had smattered the newspapers and scandalized the family to a point they feared they would not recover. But alas, when the rumors circulated, and Rebecca was believed to not be entirely at fault for the whole situation, her father had begun to breathe easy again. It had appeared that all was not lost.

But as time had gone on, Rebecca passed her twenty-second birthday and her father had yet to curate another marriage successfully. Rebecca had felt a cold distance rise between her father and herself. Henry was her only ally.

Whereas her father had tried to put the whole scandal to rest for a time, both Rebecca's paternal grandmother and society had yet to let it lie. It seemed to have been the most exciting thing that had happened in their social circles of British

Columbia in years. Perhaps it was the younger ladies, like Harriet and Anne, and their gossiping mothers that made sure the story circulated at the start of every season.

Before the scandal, Rebecca Bedford had been the most eligible and sought-after heiress in Victoria for two seasons before the marriage deal had been brokered between the astute Templeton and Bedford families. Despite not having a mother to guide her, Rebecca had secured the affection of John Templeton, allowing other young single women to have their chance at last to shine. Rebecca would have been married and out of their way had the whole thing not gone up in smoke and flames. Rebecca was sure the other young women had nothing to worry about in terms of her being a threat to their chances of securing suitable matches. But the story rose again once a year as a reminder to everyone that Rebecca Bedford had a past she could not undo with all the efforts in the world.

Not that she much cared any longer. Her sights were set, not on a successful marriage, but on uncovering the truth of her mother's past, secrets she feared her mother had taken to the grave, or perhaps had even put her there.

And she figured that was scandal enough for a lifetime.

## CHAPTER 2

*A*lbert drummed his fingers impatiently against the table in the lounge. He had been ushered into the room forty minutes earlier to wait for his meeting with Ernest Galloway. Galloway was a barrister, called to the bar seven years earlier, and practiced in the high courts. Albert had met him once two years ago, when home for the summer, and while discussing Albert's studies at Dalhousie Law School, Galloway had told him to contact him once he graduated. The man had said he would be honored to offer the son of William Harrington an apprenticeship.

It had been the motivation he needed, and he had thrown himself fully into his studies. He had even declined the invitations to travel home to meet his new niece, born sixteen months ago. Nothing had been worth the distraction. Though now that he had laid eyes on the blonde-haired blue-eyed toddler, he had to admit he wished he had spent more time with family.

Thankfully, they did not hold his absence against him. While traveling was not an issue for the Harrington family financially, the amount of time they spent pouring into their work meant that travel was a time-stealing affair. They understood his desire to remain at Dalhousie until he finished school. Now that his studies were complete, he planned to be more present, and his older brother Robert seemed happy to have him home.

When Albert had been insistent on studying law, even after their father had requested on his deathbed that he help his brother run the family business, Robert had barely spoken to him for an entire year. Marrying Caroline had softened Robert, and becoming a father to Arabella had caused him to fully reconnect with Albert. When Albert had returned home three days ago, his older brother had wrapped strong arms around him, clapping him on the back and grinning with joy at their reunion. It seemed the tide had turned, and Albert could expect to fully return to living life with the Harrington family amongst Victoria's most elite society.

Albert cared little about participating in societal

functions, but if it put him in closer proximity to his brother and sister-in-law more often, he was willing to do so. His motives were pure. Albert had not just grown in knowledge while he was away at university. He had the opportunity to hear the true Gospel of Christ, and his heart had forever changed. His brother would be appalled to know Albert had converted to Protestantism, but he knew the truth would come out soon. Robert and Caroline attended every Mass at St. Andrews. It would be apparent to them that something was amiss when he did not attend with them.

Albert was drawn out of his anxious thoughts, when at last, the door to the lounge opened and Ernest Galloway filled the open doorway.

"Mr. Harrington. It's been too long. I wish I had known you were coming today. I must be on my way soon. Did you attempt to make an appointment?"

Albert rose and extended his hand, which Galloway shook with enthusiasm. "It is great to see you, Mr. Galloway. I did, sir. Three times. I decided it would be more efficient to come in person."

Mr. Galloway grunted. "Ah. You will have to excuse my new secretary. My tight ship has gone a bit array."

"I understand, sir. Perhaps my arrival can be a solution."

The older man raised an eyebrow. "How so?"

"Well, the apprenticeship, sir," Albert faltered, seeing the blank look on the man's face. "Two years ago, you told me to come to you when I graduated. You said you would have an apprenticeship for me."

The man ran a hand over his chin. "I see. I do not recall that conversation, Albert. I'll be honest with you, I am not sure I have much available…"

Albert's heart dropped into his stomach like lead. How could this man not remember a conversation that had been replaying in Albert's head daily for the last two years?

"We were at Gosbee's summer party. I'll do anything you need, sir. I'm not above sorting files and doing research. My father taught me to make everything an opportunity to learn."

Mr. Galloway looked him up and down for what seemed an hour. Albert's face felt hot, his chest tight with anxiety. "You are the spitting image of your late father. Do you hear that often?"

"Every time I am in Victoria, sir," Albert forced a smile, wishing very much to get back to the issue at hand.

Silence took the rule of the room once more. At last, Mr. Galloway sighed.

"I cannot offer you much, Albert. Can I call you that?"

"Yes, please do, sir," Albert nodded eagerly, much less concerned about titles and names than whether he had an apprenticeship.

"If you're willing to be patient, I can start you on Mondays and Wednesdays. My secretary is off on those days. You'll fill her spot."

Albert beamed. It was something. "Thank you, sir."

"I doubt you will enjoy it much—much below your education. But if you do well, I will add to your work. Perhaps one day, you'll have an office of your own in this very building. You have an education at Dalhousie in your pocket, and if you are not a fool, you will do well. Very well indeed."

"Law school beat the fool right out of me, sir."

"Good man," Mr. Galloway turned on his heel. "I'll see you Monday. I'll arrive at nine o'clock and expect you to have a pot of coffee waiting and my itinerary on my desk. Bring your transcripts and whatever else those Dalhousie men sent with you upon graduation. I will look at them sometime in the next month."

Albert nodded, determined to be there as early as possible, and to never disappoint the man who quite possibly held the key to his future practicing law. As he left the building, he was disenchanted, to say the least. He had counted on this apprenticeship with every bit of effort he had put into school. Shamefully, he had bragged about it to a few classmates and used it as his reason for studying all hours of the night. The motive had become the source of every argument he made with himself to read one more page, write one more sentence, argue one more point. He needed to impress Mr. Galloway. He could not let him down. The man was counting on him to graduate at the top of his class, to be worthy of the apprenticeship. All the while, Mr. Galloway had likely forgotten the conversation within a couple of days. Why would he, after all, pay more mind to the second son of a deceased acquaintance?

He stood in the rain, letting it land upon his shoulders and drip from his hat. Cars and carriages rolled past, in and out of puddles on the street. While he was tempted to let his mood match the weather, he decided against it. Albert would not allow himself to be angry or defeated. He would give grace to the man and take on all fault as his own. There were a thousand other reasons to put every bit of effort into school as he had. There was something to be said about graduating with honors from Dalhousie Law School. And besides—he reasoned with himself, he did have a position under Galloway. It was something to be proud of, an achievement his other classmates could not boast of, and he would make the most of it. He strode down the sidewalk, hand out and palm up to catch the drops, marveling at the coolness against his skin as the clear water pooled in his hand.

He said a prayer of thanks as he walked, remembering how Caroline had wished for the rain, just last night, to water her withering flowers.

## CHAPTER 3

*R*ebecca returned to the library that afternoon, just as she had every afternoon for the past week. Her visit with Henry had gone well. She missed her younger brother, who spent most of his time away at school. The house was eerie and quiet with him gone, containing only the painful silence of her and her father avoiding one another while the household staff silently attempted to keep the peace.

The atmosphere had shifted dramatically with her mother's death. Bleak and gray, her father always throwing a tantrum about something, without Hannah there to lay a calming hand on his arm or to redirect emotions. It seemed the outside world and all of its problems now came freely through the door into the house. The shield was gone, slipping away with their mother into her grave eight years prior.

Rebecca's heart yearned daily for her mother. For a friendly conversation. For motherly advice. And, over the past two years, the guidance and direction her mother would have provided after the engagement with John had fallen apart. Her mother would have smoothed things over with the entire family and worked to get Rebecca back into society's good graces. But without her, Rebecca felt lost and helpless. She simply had to endure.

The library had been Hannah's favorite room in the house, and it was where Rebecca spent most of her time now. Her mother had worked tirelessly, over her twenty years of marriage to Paul Alexander Bedford, to fill the shelves with a wide assortment of books to meet each family member's interests. History and business for her husband. Science and herbology for Henry. And for Rebecca, much to her father's annoyance, her mother had lined shelves with books of law and political history. Her interests at the time of Hannah's death had been in European royal history and the deep political scandals surrounding Queen Elizabeth I and Mary Queen of Scots.

How deeply Rebecca longed for the chance to change history like those great women. Her current social sphere exhausted and irritated her to her very core. It was ever clear to her, especially after everything that had happened with John Templeton, that in her society, children were seen as a bargaining chip that, if played well, could carry great value. While Rebecca had fancied herself in love, everyone else involved in the engagement, including John, had been only concerned about the financial and societal benefits. So when John failed to give her genuine affection and wandered away to another woman, Rebecca had been cruelly awakened to reality.

Love was a fantasy that only existed in the romance novels her mother had read. And she truly wished her mother had told her that instead of having to discover it herself. She had been devastated by John's deceit and betrayal and reacted as severely as she possibly could have. The damage lingered. She had uncovered the truth of marriage. She had no interest in raising her father's social standing and therefore had no interest in marriage. She abhorred the thought of being used in such a way.

Her thoughts were occupied by other matters these days. Two weeks ago, she had uncovered eight diaries that her mother had hidden in the recesses of a bottom library shelf. They had been tucked behind a set of French dictionaries. Entirely hidden in direct reach, they had never been found, though her mother died years ago. The diaries were filled with her mother's familiar scroll.

Upon first discovery, Rebecca was sure that her mother had tried her hand at writing romance novels. The stories were entirely unfamiliar, and indeed not her mother's own records, she was quite sure at first. However, as she had continued to pour over the stories, all of which were written in a self-narrative style, her mind unwittingly began making connections to her mother's actual experiences as a young woman. She was tempted to think the young character's mother sounded strangely like her grandmother. Names of persons sounded vaguely familiar. And had not her mother also grown up in Sussex? Further similarities were found as she read on, but she was sure that her mother was simply drawing on her own experiences to write her fiction.

Then it had happened; two days ago, out of the back of the last diary she picked up to read, its pages full of shockingly detailed, passionate love, a photograph of a young man fluttered out to the carpet below Rebecca's feet.

She had stared at it for a long time, letting unknown realities be revealed. In the picture, the young man matched, detail by detail, the man written about in the diary: blonde hair, mustache, firm jaw, and military uniform.

He was real.

Which could mean only one thing in Rebecca's mind, though she had spent the following weeks attempting to dissuade herself from the truth. The stories were not fiction at all. They were real-life accounts of her mother's scandalous and sinful encounters with a young man, who by all signs, she had deeply loved. And for the past two days, Rebecca had been jittery with questions.

"Rebecca!" her father's voice boomed up the stairs, causing her to jump out of her skin. "Rebecca Elizabeth Bedford, come downstairs at once."

Rebecca rolled her eyes but hurried to her feet, setting the diaries back in their secret hideaway and rushing out into the hall. Her father was waiting at the bottom of the stairs, pocket watch in-hand, and he barely glanced up at her as she smoothed her skirts.

"I expect you to take afternoon tea in the drawing room today, Rebecca. You have used up your excuses for the week, and you must know that we cannot continue on in polite society if the woman of this house does not take guests for afternoon tea."

"Yes, Father," Rebecca agreed.

"Edwin informed me that Charlotte Thatcher sat

in that room for tea for fifteen minutes yesterday afternoon before you finally sent him down to tell her you had a headache. This is not to be borne, Rebecca."

Rebecca's mouth opened to speak, but he cut her off, and she let out a loud sigh instead.

"Your mother never missed a single afternoon tea before she was bedridden; God rest her soul. I know without a doubt that she raised you to deserve the Bedford name. Let's act like it, shall we?"

"Of course, Father." She miraculously kept her voice even despite the anger bubbling beneath the surface.

"Good. I must be off, but I will be home no later than eight this evening."

He turned to the servants, who were already extending his hat and scarf toward him. Rebecca noticed he made more eye contact with them than he did with her.

"Oh, and Rebecca," he turned toward her once more before walking out the door.

"Yes?" she looked up, desperate for him to leave her in peace.

"I accepted the invitation to the ball the Whitlow's are hosting."

"Oh," Rebecca felt herself deflate. Her father's scolding rolled off of her because of their frequent occurrence, but an evening at the Whitlow's could lower her spirits quite rapidly.

"Surely you did not think you would decline that one. Henry is home. You shall both go. It is important to me that you do."

Rebecca suspected that what her father truly implied was that Anne Whitlow would be a perfect marriage match for Henry. He meant to take every opportunity presented to see that his children married well. Rebecca had disappointed him, and now he must have set his hopes on his son to save the family by attaching themselves to the Whitlows. It had been for that very reason that she had ignored the invitation, almost to the point of rudeness. Rebecca was certain that Henry would be in a marriage before he realized what had happened, with his refusal to ruffle feathers and object to anything their father wished. And Anne Whitlow would make him miserable.

As the door closed firmly behind her father, Rebecca all but growled and trudged up the stairs. She had loved balls once upon a time, but as with everything else, John Templeton had turned that on its head. And the last thing she wanted right now was any distraction from her mother's apparent lover's mystery. That was a story she wanted to learn more about. How freeing would it be to know that her deceased mother had also felt stifled by the rules? To know that Rebecca was not the first woman in her family to be caught up in scandal?

As she sank into a chair and her eyes ran over the countless books on the shelves, she wondered just what her father knew of the whole thing. He most certainly was not the man in the picture. Even to this day, her father loved her mother deeply, but honestly, Rebecca realized she had never seen a passion between them. Only devotion and commitment.

Realizing she was alone in the house, other than household staff preparing for afternoon tea, Rebecca left the library and went to her mother's room. Her father had closed it off, forbidden anyone to remove a single thing, and only permitted a servant to go in and dust once a month. She pushed the door open and ventured in for the first time in eight months and was practically knocked down by the smell of her mother's rose-scented perfume. An ache rippled through her chest. Grief was peculiar, she supposed, brought on by the strangest of things: scents, music, the sound of a strangely familiar voice.

Rebecca's eyes scanned the room. Every item was all as it had been. Her mother's hairbrush and perfume still sat on the vanity. A bookmark remained halfway through *Jane Eyre*, her mother's favorite novel, and it sat beside the plush butter-yellow chair. In her final weeks, when her mother was too weak to leave the room, she had simply moved from bed to chair, accomplishing nothing but reading a few dozen pages before returning to the bed.

Rebecca moved toward the bed, her finger running gently over the soft pink coverlet. Tears sprang to her eyes. This had been the very place her mother had left the world. Now Rebecca stood there wondering what had gone on behind the eyes of that beloved woman.

She must put emotions aside; there was a mystery to solve. Her hand reached toward the night table drawer. This was the place Rebecca had always known her mother to keep her diaries. It was why the secret stash was such a shocking discovery. They had been hidden with purpose and care.

The drawer was deep, but inside was only one diary. The last one her mother had kept. It had not been filled, and Rebecca had read it once already, the year after her mother's passing. It had been long before she had fallen out of favor with her father, and when she returned from finishing school that summer, he had let her read it. He had hoped it would give her peace, because it had for him. At the time, it had been an intensely emotional experience for her, reading her mother's last written words. But it had helped her in her grief, and she had bonded deeply with her father over it.

Oh, how things had changed.

Rebecca thought hard for a moment about where her mother would have put the other diaries. She had kept one for every year of her marriage. And for eight years before that as well. She remembered being scolded once for playing under the bed and getting her Easter dress ripped on the wood box kept under there. If her memory served her correctly, it was where the other nineteen diaries would be found.

She glanced over her shoulder to assure the door was closed and no one would witness her crawling about on the ground in all her lady-like glory. Down on hands and knees, cheek pressed to the rug, and bed-skirt halfway over her head, Rebecca stretched out her arm and reached for the box. Her fingers grasped the leather strap, and she gave a good tug. With great force against the friction of the high-threaded carpeting, the box relented and slid toward her. It was long, and she moved out of its way as it came toward her. In total, it spanned the length of the bed but was considerably narrow, just the size of a book, specially made for that specific spot and purpose. It was covered in a thick layer of dust.

Apparently, the maid missed this while dusting, but running her hand over it revealed the finely polished wood. The hinges creaked in protest as she lifted the wooden lid.

The diaries were in order, earliest to latest in years, but Rebecca was most interested in the first edition. She wanted to piece together the story from that final secret diary to this one; her mother's first year of marriage. As she opened it carefully, so as not to damage it, her eyes landed on the first entry date.

*2 February 1887*

*Mother was pleased to inform me this morning that a marriage offer has been made for me. She seems quite satisfied with what Father was able to accomplish on behalf of the family, but I find myself completely cynical within.*

*Is it that the match will still provide them significant financial gain, despite my considerable deficiencies, or the fact that I will be out from under their roof where I have been threatening their reputations that pleases her so? While I know I have put them through numerous trials of late, I still feel as though I am put out of the house. Mother tells me I am dramatic and sensitive.*

*They are sending me as far away as possible. This new*

*husband of mine, one Paul Alexander Bedford, resides not here in this county, nor even in this country, but in Victoria, British Columbia. They desire to remove me to a whole new continent. And for this reason, following the wedding in May, when my new husband and his parents will arrive to take me back with them, I highly doubt I will ever lay eyes on my parents again.*

*And Mother practically said good riddance as she announced it all over breakfast, while Father lowered his paper just enough to gauge my reaction. Seeing as how they broke the stalemate of silence that has ruled this house since my return, I only hope I put on enough of a performance to please them in their valiant efforts to save me.*

The entry was dated an entire year after the last entry of the secret diaries. And as Rebecca opened each of the others to find the missing year, she came up empty. Where was the missing year of her mother's life? How did she go from passionately in love with one man, to married to Paul Bedford and placed at the top of Victoria's society?

She barely needed another flicker of mystery to add fuel to her search. For underneath the last journal, was a thin envelope laced with a whitish powdery substance. She was clueless as to what it was.

Rebecca needed answers. Were the stories of how

her parents had met, how it had been a fairy tale, all a lie? Why had her grandparents sent her mother so far away? What had she done to deserve it? How had the young woman, who seemed so completely appalled by society, become the mother Rebecca had known; a woman who was the epitome of grace and social wisdom?

She had no idea where to begin searching for answers. It would require research and investigative skills she did not possess. And in her world run by men and so controlled by her father, she would not be able to step a foot toward the answers without him reigning down on her with all the fury he could muster. He would see it as disrespect and demand she let her mother rest in peace.

Rebecca could not. She would never find peace within herself with all the mystery swirling around in her brain. She would need to hire someone to seek out the answers for her. Someone she could trust to keep it quiet and who had training in such tasks. Someone she knew well. And she knew exactly where to find such a person. Sure to be in attendance at the Whitlow ball was Anne's cousin, Albert Harrington. She had grown up with him and had barely paid him any attention at all. He had been reserved and uninteresting until he had his own moment of rebelling against family wishes and going off to Dalhousie instead of assuming a role in the family business. He had always had an eye on her, after all. And if he still did, she was sure she could convince him to help her.

With renewed purpose, Rebecca returned everything to its place of origin and left the room to discuss with her lady's maid, Alice, what was to be done about a dress for the ball.

## CHAPTER 4

It was not until Albert was standing in the ballroom of the Whitlow's massive and ornate home, surrounded by those whom he had grown up with, that he realized just how long he had been away. His surroundings during his final years at Dalhousie had remained unchanged; the same people, the same library and studying spots, the same classrooms, professors, and residence. He had so rarely looked up from his books; he realized now, as he looked into so many familiar and yet different faces, that his image had shifted quite a lot too.

He had grown into what had at one time been a tall and lanky body. His shoulders and torso had filled out to surpass the bony features he had once had. Thick brown hair lay back in slight curls, an unruly mess he did his best to tame. He kept his beard and mustache closely trimmed, not wanting to appear unkept and unprofessional. His dear sister-in-law told him that he had become one of the most handsome men in the ballroom. She had even teased that if he did not end the year with a young woman on his arm and half of them completely stricken with jealousy, she would be completely shocked.

Albert hoped Caroline was not planning to work the magic some married women claimed to have in the art of matchmaking. He had often wondered why every woman in love considered themselves suddenly an expert on love itself and thought they should proceed to pair up every other single person they knew. It had baffled him beyond belief and, now that he feared he would be on the receiving end of such efforts, scared him a bit. Yet now, as he glanced across the room at Robert and Caroline over the rim of his wine glass, he saw them and two young ladies looking right at him, Caroline smiling excitedly.

"Oh, dear," Albert muttered, rolling his eyes and turning on his heel.

The dancing was just getting started, and Albert was aware of how rude he would appear if he spent the entire evening standing to the side and refusing to dance. He simply hoped he could wait awhile; participate in some conversations, reacquaint himself with old friends, and perhaps find some non-threatening ladies to spend a few dances with. It wasn't that Albert was against the idea of marriage. His parents had a wonderful marriage while they were both alive, and now Robert and Caroline were happily married. But it had instilled in Albert the need to marry only for love, not for financial, social, or political gain. The fact that he was not to inherit his family fortune freed him to do exactly that; find a woman who would complement his own traits, one with whom there would be mutual respect, adoration, and love.

He would not settle for anything less.

There was a flurry of activity across the room as Anne Whitlow, clad in a bright red dress sure to catch the attention of everyone in attendance, flew across the room toward the entrance. The high pitch of her voice could be equated with the screech of a hawk, and it took great willpower on Albert's part to not plug his ears.

"Henry! I was worried you weren't coming!"

The room was not overly large, but Albert's eyes widened at the lack of decorum. There was absolutely no reason he should have overheard her greeting a guest from his location. But his mind was diverted almost immediately when he realized who had caused Anne to show such a lack of propriety.

Walking through the door was Henry Bedford, son of the third wealthiest man in Victoria. And just behind him, the woman who had been surrounded by so much scandal over the last two years that Albert had caught wind of it from his brother in a letter to Dalhousie. The fact that Robert, the man who ceremoniously stood above the ways of gossip and rumor, had written about it, made Albert realize he was likely missing quite the uproar at home.

Rebecca Bedford carried herself as bravely and proudly as ever, unfazed by Anne snubbing her with her shoulder, or the attention immediately on her. She had been through a lot over the past few years, and though it was clear everyone wished she would simply disappear from the face of the earth, she remained just as she always had been; the most beautiful woman in the room. He knew she was also the wealthiest, and that was the real reason all the others hated her. She was everything they wanted to be. Her deep chestnut-colored hair was done up in the most recent fashion, and she wore a royal blue dress that perfectly accentuated her features. Her skin was alabaster, her facial structure almost completely symmetrical, and her eyes a soft green. His heart raced and he swallowed, recognizing that feeling he had every time she walked in the room, though it had been absent for so long.

People were intent on avoiding her, leaving her path wide open and allowing him to take her in completely. She was destined to spend the rest of her life living on the rims of this world, a fact that made Albert's heart ache with empathy for her. She would live comfortably but Albert could not imagine the feeling of being completely unwanted by everyone in their society. It was a cruel business, being scorned in love. Albert swallowed back the temptation to hate John Templeton.

John Templeton had never been a close friend to Albert. They were the same age and had grown up together, but Albert and John had always had very different personalities. It was not until they were in their mid-adolescent years that Albert had begun to fully realize how differently they looked at the world, but they had always been like night and day. John was larger than life, rambunctious, and made a joke around every turn. He had been the object of every girl's affection and the center of every social occasion. His father had never checked his behavior, never punished him, and he had grown spoiled.

Albert, forever the rule follower, as well as a shy and studious boy, had often stood to the side, shaking his head in disapproval. Often, he had been punished by his parents just for being in the same place at the same time when John had caused a ruckus. And Albert had watched with aversion as the young man settled into the pursuit of Rebecca Bedford, sure it would end in disaster.

The union had been hoped for since the infancy of John and Rebecca. It was a power match between the Templeton and Bedford families that would unite their fortunes and center the couple at the height of British Columbia's society. And for that reason, Paul Alexander Bedford had turned a blind eye to John's behavior and placed his daughter's hand into that reckless young man's grip. And Rebecca's reputation had been destroyed, though that had come much later.

Albert remembered that last summer he was home with vivid detail. In marriage, Robert had grown stale and pestered him with advice and commands, and Albert had rebelled against his elder brother that year. He had spent his time with the society that he had previously found immature and annoying. But that summer, he had been endlessly caught up in the scene unfolding before him, like a train-wreck he could not look away from. It had been the beginning of the end for John and Rebecca's engagement, although he had not known at the time that it would all come crashing down four months later.

One day, the usual group of eleven had gone to a

picnic on the coast. They were a loud bunch, and Albert shifted between enjoying it and being overwhelmed. As always, John had led the group from the front, Rebecca's hand firmly clasped in his. Not everyone in the group was paired off. In fact, Rebecca and John had been the only pair promised to one another. Maybe that had been a part of the downfall. John had not been ready for the commitment being asked of him, and he should have never claimed to be.

Albert had watched, fist curled, as John had pushed Rebecca too far. The whole group had been lounging around in the midday sun, talking and eating the fill of their picnic baskets. Harriett and Anne had chatted in whispers and giggles for most of the day, while Henry, Rebecca's younger brother, slept nearby, hat drawn down over his eyes. They sat away from the older group a bit, meaning Henry missed the entirety of the ordeal. Ethan and Tom had been in their height of enjoyment all day. Three women, Cynthia, Isabella, and Juliet, to two men. Albert was not at all a concern to them, as he was too shy for the girls to notice. And Anne and Harriett had been like annoying little sisters. The two men flirted endlessly that day, and the older girls had fallen for it in every possible way. John had looked on in what Albert could merely guess was jealousy. He was tied to one woman for the rest of eternity, and while she had clearly loved John with everything that she was, Rebecca was anything but a silly flirt.

They had all had far too much wine that afternoon, and Albert watched out of the corner of his eye as John sat up and leaned close to Rebecca's ear. She had blushed crimson but smiled and whispered back. The next thing Albert knew, he was watching John lean over Rebecca and trail his lips behind her ear and down her neck. His fingers had worked furiously to push the fabric of her dress off her shoulder, while Rebecca squirmed away. Finally, she stuck both arms out and pushed him off.

"John!" she had exclaimed in admonishment. "Stop it! You are drunk!"

It had all unfolded in less than ten seconds, and Albert could not move past the shock of what was happening and step in. He had then watched a furious John scramble to his feet, glaring down at her. He had kicked his toe at their laundry basket, drawing the attention of everyone but Henry, Anne, and Harriett.

"Don't be such a prude, Beth," he had seethed as Ethan and Tom laughed. "I have a right, you know."

She had simply turned her head away. And for the rest of the day, John seemed intent on punishing her. He openly flirted with Cynthia and Isabella right in front of her, both of whom allowed him to let his hand linger on their arms or hold their gaze with a suggestive smile. Albert had been disgusted by the whole thing and avoided the group after that, all too happy to return to school and his studies. Robert had written him later that fall to tell him that the engagement was off and John had run away to London to elope with a pregnant Cynthia. He had not been as surprised as he should have been by the news. His heart had been broken for Rebecca and the pain he knew she was enduring in the wake of such destruction. He remembered feeling torn, knowing he had a chance at last to swoop in and love her the way she had deserved. But he was committed to his studies and plans. He had to finish. There was no other option but to put her as far out his mind as possible. He had thought of Rebecca often since then and prayed she was doing well and healing, but never allowing his mind to travel past that point.

Albert tried to reconcile the memories with the woman who stood so brilliantly in the doorway now. As everyone attempted to ignore her presence, she visibly heaved a great sigh. Albert saw Henry look over his shoulder at her, caught a glimpse of the tight smile that passed between them before Anne whisked Henry away to dance. Albert added a conversation with her to the list of things he wanted to accomplish that evening as her eyes landed directly on him. He froze. And then his heart began to race as she headed boldly toward him.

He glanced around, certain she was walking toward someone else. But as she drew closer, it became apparent that he was the one she had centered her attention on.

"Miss Bedford," he bowed when she reached him. "It is wonderful to see you again."

She smiled warmly, and he felt the luckiest man in the whole room to be the one to receive it. "You as well, Mr. Templeton. Henry told me you had come home."

"It is good to be here. I've missed this place."

"Really? What about it?"

Rebecca seemed like she disbelieved him, and he knew why. She hated this place as much as it hated her. Albert shrugged.

"This is home. No matter where I go, this will always be the place where I grew up. The place where memories of my parents burn the strongest. And now it's where my beautiful niece is."

She smiled, though it seemed a bit half-hearted. "Family can be a wonderful thing."

He followed her eyes to where Henry danced

with Anne, his face bright and happy. "Henry has certainly grown."

"He's become a man," Rebecca nodded. "I hardly know when it happened, though I suspect it's largely my fault. He acts more like an older brother these days than a younger one."

Albert laughed, recalling a memory. "Do you remember that last summer I was home, when Ethan and Harriett and Anne jumped into the harbor at The Empress? Anne's dress was so heavy she started to sink, and who else went in after her, but—"

"Henry in his new suit?" she giggled. "The poor boy, his suit was ruined, and no matter how heroic Anne found him that day, Father scolded him harshly."

"I was half inclined to think she was faking," Albert leaned closer.

Rebecca looked surprised and put her hand to her chest. "Truly? And I thought I was the only one who doubted her every motive."

"Well, her motive tonight seems clear," Albert said, watching the young couple, beautifully matched, dance around the room. "They look good together. Happy."

She scoffed.

"You disagree?"

"No. I just wish with everything in me that it wasn't true."

Albert and Rebecca eyed one another for a moment. Albert was not at all surprised by their easy banter. She had always been easy to talk to, though other girls had often said she was far too open for polite company. He liked that about her. There was never a question of what she was thinking. No guessing games. It spoke volumes to the rising lawman in him.

"Pardon me for saying so, but you seemed to be on quite the mission when you saw me."

"You don't think I just wanted to say hello to an old friend?" she asked it with a teasing smile, not for a moment denying the truth of his statement. "No, you are correct. There's a very personal matter I'd like to discuss with you. Perhaps over a dance, away from listening ears?"

He nodded, curiosity piqued. Albert spotted the doors open to the balcony and offered her his arm. He escorted her out, not unaware that they were under watchful eyes. Normally he would not be so forward. But this was Rebecca Bedford standing before him, seeking out a chance to talk to him, and he cared little what they thought of him. They had disowned the best woman among them, so what could he want with their good opinion?

Outside, the cold air was a welcome change of atmosphere. The sky was littered with stars, and they could hear the music well enough.

"May I have this dance, Miss Bedford?" he held out a hand.

"You may," she smiled, slipping her hand into his. She wasted no time broaching her topic. "You studied law at Dalhousie?"

"I did," he nodded, their feet moving together. "Graduated top of my class."

"Well done," she congratulated him. "So you practice law now?"

"One day...for now I am working for Mr. Ernest Galloway."

Her eyes widened, letting him know she was familiar with the name. But he was admittedly having trouble focusing on the conversation. Rebecca Bedford had been the apple of his eye through most of his life. His shyness had meant she had barely noticed him, and her family trained her to look only toward John Templeton from the moment she had been old enough to consider such things. She had never been a real option as the object of his affection, but he had always admired her from afar, mesmerized by her beauty and personality. Now, having her in his arms, completely alone with her on the Whitlow's balcony, he was in awe. It seemed hard to believe it was truly happening.

"But...well, what I am wondering is if you were educated on how to investigate things."

"Crime?" he arched an eyebrow.

"No. History."

"I am not following you."

She chewed her lip, and he swallowed, his breath hitching in his throat. "Mr. Harrington, I would like to hire you to investigate something for me. But it must remain confidential. Not even my family can know of it. Can I trust you to keep my confidence?"

Rebecca Bedford wanted to take him into her confidence? He would have to peel himself from the surface of the moon in a few hours, he was sure. "Of course. That is my duty."

She nodded, but still seemed unsure. He gave her time as the music changed into a soft ballad. At last, she took a deep breath.

"I recently discovered private journals, hidden in a secret place in our family library. They were my mother's. At first, I thought they were filled with the romantic silliness a teenage girl can often get into when she's read too many romance novels. But they became more and more risqué, quite shocking really, and I began to notice similarities to things I knew to be true about my mother's young life in Great

Britain. As I began to wonder how much of what I was reading was a true account, a picture of a young man, the man I'm sure was being described in the journal, fell to my feet. I realized it was true. All of it. My mother had many secrets, including a premarital relationship."

Albert was sure his eyes were the size of saucers as the story poured out of her. Yet he remained silent, waiting for her to divulge her reason for sharing it all with him.

"There is a year missing between her last secret journal and the ones she kept in her bedroom. Over the course of that year, my mother went from being passionately in love with this mysterious gentleman, to engaged to my father in a marriage arranged by my grandfathers. And I want to know what happened during that missing year. How did her life change so dramatically? And who is the man?"

"Why?" Albert asked. "Why do you want to know? It seems to me that pursuing that line of inquiry could bring about disaster and pain. What would you do with the information if you had it?"

She stepped away from him, out of his arms, and moved to the balcony. She looked out over the Whitlow's extensive gardens, lit up by lamps along the walking paths. When she remained silent for quite some time, he moved to stand beside her.

"I have to know," she admitted. "I have to know who my mother was. I've spent my entire life living in her shadow. My father tells me every day how much I've fallen short. And if that's my fate, to be compared to her, I want to know the truth. If my mother could survive whatever happened to her... perhaps the loss of great love... and still have gone on to live such a grand life, maybe... "

Her voice trailed, and he saw her shudder.

"Maybe what?" he prompted, his voice soft.

"Maybe I can survive too."

Silence hung between them, the weight of it pressing in on them. Staring at her, noting the sheer desperation in her voice, he saw for the first time that she was also putting on a façade. Underneath that proud and graceful composure, she was on the verge of falling apart. She was suffocating under lies and questions about her identity. She needed a center. He had the ability to give it to her, knowing it needed to come from something other than the answers she sought.

"I can come by during calling hours tomorrow," he said at last. "I would like to see the journals. I would like to assist you in any way I can in finding the answers you seek."

"I'll pay you," she turned to him, her features schooled into composure.

"We can discuss that another time," he said.

"This would mean a great deal to me."

Albert nodded and was about to say something else when gasps were heard from inside, and the music ground to a halt. Albert and Rebecca exchanged curious glances, wondering what they had missed. They moved back indoors, Albert just behind her, and he nearly ran over her as she came to an abrupt stop, frozen in place. He looked beyond her to the doorway where none other than John Templeton stood, an amused smirk written across his face as always. As Victoria's highest society took in their first sight of him in two years, their eyes slowly began to shift to Rebecca to take in her reaction.

Henry at once crossed the room, abandoning Anne, and wrapped his arm around his sister.

"What is he doing here?" Albert heard her whisper to her younger brother.

"I don't know," Henry said. "I did not know he had returned. But I am certain the Whitlows did not invite him. He's a disgrace."

Henry tried to set her in motion, but her feet were cemented to the floor.

"Come, Rebecca," Henry said firmly. "It's time to go."

Albert watched them exit the room—Henry the

only thing standing between John and Rebecca as they passed him, and the whole party watching as if some great Shakespearean play was being acted out in front of them. He recalled in full force why he had stayed away for as long as he had. The whole of the room was suddenly despicable to him, and he took his leave not long after, snubbing his shoulder at the disgusting sight of John Templeton. Manners could be reserved for another day, and perhaps never for that particular man.

## CHAPTER 5

*R*ebecca was anxiously awaiting Albert's arrival the Sunday afternoon after the party. Her foot tapped against the rug as she sat on the sofa in the parlor, attempting to keep her hands busy with needlework. The awareness of her mother's journals hidden in the piano bench was practically burning a hole in her brain. She wondered if Albert Harrington would find them as mysterious as she did. Would he find it worth his time for the small sum she was offering? Or would he dismiss it as a fantasy she had built up in her mind?

She had determined to put the arrival of John Templeton firmly out of her mind. It had been so shocking she could almost convince herself it had been nothing but a nightmare. It certainly was not worth her time or the nerves that had been bubbling inside of her ever since. Instead, she chose to remember her conversation on the balcony with Albert, replaying it over and over in her thoughts. It had been a long time since anyone had looked at her with such kindness, or had really stopped to look at her at all, and she was certain that was why she had felt such warmth spread through her when he had.

The bell rang, and she sat up straighter, heart racing with excitement. She felt she was in a Sherlock Holmes tale and hoped desperately she would be the Watson to Albert's Sherlock. At least in the way of being his assistant, she amended mentally, blushing at the mere thought of sharing rent of an apartment with a man.

And it was with a highly flushed face that she turned to see the butler, Edwin, hurry into the room.

"Miss Rebecca, I am not sure I should allow this person in to see you. It is a man."

"Well, it is not as if I will be closing the door, Edwin. Any of the staff may walk in at any moment," she shrugged at him. "Let Mr. Harrington in. You're rude to make him wait, and I have business matters to discuss with him."

"It is not Mr. Harrington at the door, Miss Rebecca."

"Oh! Well, who is it?"

The old butler swallowed. "It's Mr. Templeton. John Templeton."

Rebecca was immediately on her feet. "Well, of course, don't let him in here! Tell him I do not wish to see him."

Edwin bowed. "Yes, Miss. As you wish."

Rebecca waited until he left the room and then sank weakly back to the sofa. How dare he come here. What could he possibly have to say to her?

As she listened she could not hear Edwin's words, but she immediately heard John's response.

"She isn't ill, or you would not have gone into the parlor to ask. Let me pass."

"No, sir," she heard Edwin's voice and words this time, more assertive. "She does not wish to see you, and quite frankly, neither do I."

Rebecca paled as she remembered the last time John had been here; he had made Edwin go into the street to find the engagement ring Rebecca had angrily thrown out the library window. The butler, who had served the family faithfully for years, had been horribly humiliated and mistreated by John that day, as had she.

"You have no business speaking to me that way!" she heard John's angry reply. "Rebecca! Rebecca, tell him to let me in!"

She rose angrily, hearing him shout through the

house for her as if it belonged to him. She crossed to the French doors, arms folded across her chest as she peered out into the entryway. He towered over Edwin and looked up at her, hat still on his head because Edwin had refused to take it. His face was red with anger.

"What do you want?" she asked, her tone tight.

"I just want to speak with you," his voice softened considerably. "Please."

"And what will you do if I refuse?"

"Return each day until you allow me in," John said. "I'm determined."

She sighed heavily and waved her hand to dismiss Edwin. "You have five minutes. Less if you infuriate me."

Edwin stepped out of the way but refused to take John's hat. John threw it to the floor and followed Rebecca as she retreated into the parlor. She remained standing and did not offer for him to sit, nor did she call for tea.

"Mr. Templeton," she acknowledged with a quick nod of her head. "Your time has started already."

"Mr. Templeton?" he laughed deeply. "Upon my word, Rebecca. Have we regressed far enough to lose our familiarity with one another?"

"There was a time when I loved you," she

reminded him. "But you made sure to put a stop to that."

"Really, my dear. If you love me no longer, where does this passionate anger come from, I wonder?"

She glared at him. "Do not put on false airs with me, Mr. Templeton. I know your true nature. Your lack of Christian charity, your ability to spin webs of lies and lead people along. And let us not forget your ability to make everyone so blindly love you."

"None of them ever mattered to me, Rebecca. Only you."

"You have so easily forgotten the woman for which you threw away our future? You so easily claim it has only been me while you flew weekly to Cynthia's arms?"

Rebecca knew better than to bring up Cynthia. The girl had died in childbirth not long after John had taken her to Europe. By the stricken look on his face, she knew bringing her up caused great pain to him.

"Can we not let her rest in peace instead of bringing up that whole business?"

"It is your fault she's dead," Rebecca reminded him. "Bringing your child into the world...a child that should not have existed. You should feel the shame of that every day."

It was a cruel thing to say, and she was surprised

such a thing had come out of her mouth. She watched his face, certain she had gone too far, but she would not apologize. After the pain she had endured at his hand, she felt she had just cause to remind him of his sins.

"So, this is what you've become? Bitter in your unforgiveness of me? Your pride and your jealousy destroyed us, not my actions alone. You practically pushed me toward her."

"Pushed you toward her?" Rebecca shouted.

"Yes. If you had not been such a prude and shirked away from your duties as my beloved," she shot a glare at him for calling her such a thing. "Do not pretend to be so innocent. I was young. I made mistakes trying to satisfy needs you refused to meet."

"We weren't married yet!" She reminded him. "I was better than that. Than *her*."

"Yes," he nodded. "I see that now. But, Beth, you are the one I loved. I need you to believe that."

"You never loved me. You asked for my hand simply because of your father, and because the whole of Victoria expected you to do so. Not because you wanted it, or wanted me, for that matter, but because you had to."

"That isn't true."

"It is true. And I'll tell you what else is true, Mr. Templeton. I'm quite done with the whole thing."

"Yes, you have made that quite clear."

"I speak of more than our relationship. I speak of society as a whole. I half expect to be cast out at any time. I've gone against everything that could ever have been wanted of me by you, by society, by my parents. I refused to marry you because you were with another woman, because she was carrying your child, and yet I am the one who has taken the brunt of the fall. They want nothing to do with me."

"Let me fix this… " he pleaded. "We are supposed to be together, Rebecca! We always were."

She could not help the tears that came then, nor settle the nausea that rolled over her. It was like she was back in this same room two years ago, breaking off the engagement all over again. She had heard the rumors like everyone else, confronted John in a room full of people, and then the next day he had come to make amends. Except she had taken none of it and at last ripped the ring off of her finger and hurled it out the window in a fit of rage. It still hurt, and she was surprised by that fact because she had thought she had done so well at moving on.

"Beth," he spoke so softly, in the tone he always used to get his way, and bent on one knee before her, taking her hand in between both of his. "Come away with me, darling. Let's just forget these past years ever happened and start afresh. We were always meant for one another. I'm returning to London in the fall, and then onto the continent. We can be gone long enough for everyone to forget this ever happened."

"I do not want to trade this society for another just as dull and proud. And I refuse to walk around on your arm, pretending for another moment of my life."

"What choice do you have? No one else will take you."

Rebecca ripped her hand from his, fire on her tongue. "Don't! Don't pretend you are better than me! Don't insist that my only hope is with you. Don't pretend to be performing some grand gesture by offering to rescue me from what society considers such a lowly state when it is your fault alone that I am in this state at all. You, John Templeton, were once everything I thought I could want. And I would have loved you to the best of my ability, blindly as it was. But you—you threw me away."

"I threw you away?" he thundered, rising back to his full height. "I seem to recall begging on my hands and knees while you dared to throw my ring out the open window into the streets below! I swear, Rebecca, if you weren't so high and mighty... if your pride were not bigger than your station in life! I would not have married her. I would have helped her parents send her quietly away. We could have gone on to a happy marriage.

"And let us not forget, I was doing your father a favor by asking for your hand. Speculation was back then that he was close to losing it all, and a partnership with my family would have saved his financial status. And now! Now, as I stop to take notice of you, to offer for you once more, you toss me away. Do you not realize what a mistake you are making? You could have more wealth than you imagine and nary care in the world, and yet you throw it away because my wandering eyes injured your pride over two years ago!"

"A favor?" she screeched. "That's what you saw it as? And I suppose you think these romantic declarations will win me back? No. No, John, not in this lifetime. You had me, and you looked elsewhere, and now you have lost."

"Come, Rebecca," he laughed haughtily, "Where are these Christian principles you took care to remind me of? I've confessed my sin, done my penance."

"I don't recall you asking for my forgiveness, however," she told him. "Rather, you asked for me to turn away while you would continue to have affairs and while you gave money to Cynthia and your child. You assured me that it was completely normal for a man to have mistresses and that I would come to make peace with it in time. You never once asked me to forgive you. And I will say the same thing to you now as I did then. I will not be second to another woman, Mr. Templeton. I will be the love of a man's life or not at all. I will *not* be second."

He stared at her, his face turning up in a smirk of amusement and disbelief.

"What is it that you want, anyway?" she asked, trying to make sense of why he was going through such effort. "My inheritance?"

"Don't do me the disservice!" he argued. "I cared for you. I still do. And I have more to offer to this match now than I did before. It would advance your position further, and I daresay, my new connections could do your father a lot of good."

"Do not mention my father. He is ten times the man in every way that you will ever be. You are not fit to even stand in this house."

She was certain his eyes could not roll further back in his head. "Well, that is where you are wrong, my dear, for it is your father who first contacted me when I returned. He is the one who told me you would be at that ball last night, and he permitted me to call on you today."

Rebecca felt the sting of betrayal in her heart but tried her best to hide it from her face as John stepped far too close to be appropriate. She remembered her father telling her that her reaction to the whole ordeal was dramatic and embarrassing. He had insisted she do her best to put it out of her mind and marry John. Inside a war had waged in her ever since, desperately wishing someone would tell her that she was justified in her anger. She could not understand why everyone seemed to think she would have been better off marrying this man. He was despicable. And she was determined not to crumble, even though the thought of having her father look at her with pride again was a temptation she could barely withstand.

His breath was hot on her face when he spoke. "I will not offer for your hand again, Rebecca. This is your last chance to return to the life you should have had."

"I wouldn't go back to you for the whole world if I could not have love, John," Rebecca squared her shoulders, refusing to shrink under his attempt to intimidate her. "If my two years apart from you have taught me nothing else, it is that I will never settle for less than to be completely loved and cherished. It would be the death of me."

––––––

Albert heard the shouting going on the moment he entered the house. He looked with concern toward the butler.

"She has a guest," the butler muttered, his disdain evident on his face. "Mr. Templeton is here."

Albert tensed, the hair standing up on the back of his neck. "*John* Templeton?"

The butler nodded and Albert put a hand on his arm, asking if she was alone with him. When the butler confirmed his suspicions, Albert demanded that he be taken to them immediately. The doors were open, and Albert saw John towering over her, Rebecca stubbornly staring him down. Her face was red, but John's was redder. They did not touch, but Albert could practically feel the fire radiating out of the room. It seemed Rebecca was holding her ground, though Albert was still appalled that John had dared show his face there.

The butler cleared his throat in the open doorway, but neither of them flinched at the sound.

"Mr. Harrington to see you, Miss Rebecca," he spoke softly but clearly, and Rebecca turned her head to see Albert standing just behind the butler. He recognized the relief that washed over her features.

"Oh, Albert," Rebecca beamed, moving toward

him and looping her arm through his. "You remember Mr. Templeton, don't you, darling?"

"I do," he spoke, his eyebrows furrowed together as he looked down at her in surprise. It did not take him more than a second to realize she was taking advantage of his presence to send John on his way as quickly as possible. He raised his eyes toward John, forcing himself to meet his gaze. "Hello, John. I am surprised to see you here."

"Albert," John's voice was tight as he took in the scene before him, Rebecca practically draped across Albert.

The two men shook hands, and Rebecca smiled up at Albert before turning a daring smirk toward John.

"Mr. Templeton was just leaving," Rebecca said. "You will have to excuse him, Albert."

"Of course," Albert bowed his head at John, swallowing under the harsh threats being silently hurled his way. They were two men in war for one woman, Albert knew in that moment, and Albert had won this battle.

"Goodbye, Mr. Templeton," Rebecca said, her voice so sweet, and yet laced with venom. Albert was glad not to be the one on the receiving end of such a tone. "Have a pleasant day."

John let out a disgusted breath of air through his

nostrils and exited the room with haste, slamming the door in his wake, causing Rebecca to flinch at the sound. She immediately removed herself from Albert's side, putting distance between them. He immediately was aware of the cold that swept over him at her absence.

"Please, come in and be seated," Rebecca told him. "Would you like tea?"

He took a moment to answer and made no move toward a chair. He needed a moment to be as far away from her as possible while he mentally sorted through what had happened. "Yes, thank you."

She set about making the tea, but when she picked up the cup and saucer, her hands were shaking so severely that they clinked together noisily. She did quick work on handing the tea over to him, where he then sat down, his eyes still on her.

"I apologize for my behavior, Mr. Harrington. John—I mean, Mr. Templeton had quite outstayed his welcome, and I did not know how else to encourage him to leave. But I used you, and I apologize."

A deep blush had risen upon her cheeks, and she did not make eye contact. The maid came fluttering in with a plate of shortbread, giving them both a reprieve. When she had exited again, Albert spoke at last.

"May I ask what the nature of his visit was?" he asked. "Forgive me for saying so, but you seem distressed."

Rebecca smiled softly and lowered herself to the sofa. "Not distressed, but furious. That man is quite possibly the last person on earth I ever want to see. I am assuming you may have heard pieces of the gossip surrounding my failed engagement with him?"

"I have," he said, feeling shame rise up in him. "My brother had a business deal fall through with the Templeton family after John ran off with that woman."

She sighed heavily.

"Why was he here, Miss Bedford? Can I assist you in some way?"

"No, of course not. You did quite enough by playing along with me for a few moments. He came to propose once more and proceeded to tell me that I was making a mistake to refuse him."

Albert's eyes widened, and his mouth fell open. "You must be joking."

"I wish I was," she smiled, and then laughed softly. "So apparently, I am now destined to be an old maid, because he has declared that was the last offer of marriage I will ever receive."

"He's a fool," Albert proclaimed.

She nodded. "That is what Henry always says. But Mr. Templeton could be right. The whole scandal has ruined me, and my father agrees with him. He apparently encouraged Mr. Templeton to come today. I am set to inherit, and my father only thinks of loss and gain when he looks at me. I have failed to advance him and Henry through a good marriage. And when my father hears I turned down a match with the Templeton family once more, he may, in fact, disinherit me and turn to Henry as his only hope."

"I highly doubt that, Miss Bedford. What happened with Mr. Templeton was not at all your fault. And forgive me for saying so, but if your father thinks you will never make another match, or that your only value comes from the ability to do so, he is a fool as well."

At that moment, Rebecca seemed desperate to move on to another topic.

"Come," Rebecca smiled and moved to pull the journals from where she had hidden them in the piano bench. "I would like to show you the real reason for your visit. Though please keep your voice low. I do not want the staff gossiping about this."

For the next half hour, they avoided the topic of the disliked Templeton heir, and Rebecca showed Albert the journals, the photograph, and the notes she had taken so far as she had attempted to piece clues together about the identity of the mystery man her mother had once truly loved. He was intrigued by it all, this window into Rebecca's familial past, and glad to have an excuse to spend the time with her. He looked at the photograph multiple times, flipped through the pages, trying to come up with a sense of direction.

"There's something else," she told him, going back to the piano bench once more.

From amongst her sheets of music, which were evidently well worn, she withdrew the envelope. He eyed it curiously as she handed it to him, peered inside, and paled a bit at the sight of the white powder within.

"Where was this?" he asked.

"In her nightstand. Father forbids anything to be cleaned out from the room. He once dismissed a staff member after catching them in there a few weeks after my mother died. Since, he has only allowed the room to be dusted under my watchful eyes so that nothing is moved. I am the only one with a key besides my father. So, it has been there since before her death."

His brows furrowed. He suspected he knew what it was but had no wish to claim it and bring undue pain.

"What do you think it is?" Rebecca asked him.

"I cannot be sure, and I do not want to speculate. But I know where to take it to find out. I will bring you answers about it soon. Would you mind if I return at the same time on Tuesday? I should know more by then."

It was a long three days away, but he wanted to have answers before he returned. He knew she needed them, and he wanted her to trust that he was capable of finding them. "That would be fine. However, I must warn you to be careful. Being seen coming here and being in my company could lead you to be pulled into my life, living amongst the shadows of gossip. Your own reputation is at stake."

"Well, you might have thought that before you alluded to John Templeton that there was some sort of relationship between us."

His tone was a bit snappier than he intended, and she blushed and rushed to apologize before she noticed the teasing smile turning up the corners of his lips. She smiled, causing his own smile to widen.

"Worry not, Miss Bedford. I suspect being seen together would not do harm, but only good."

She cocked her head to the side as she considered it. He was in danger of letting her know he had deep feelings for her. Otherwise, why would he go along with a façade that seemed beneficial only to her, both making her seem alluring to others again, and keeping John Templeton from making any further attempts? It would damage his own reputation, but it was a risk he was very willing to take. As he had discovered at the ball, the opinions of others mattered little in comparison to her.

## CHAPTER 6

*A*lbert had a full first day that Monday. He had arrived at Galloway's office at eight, made a pot of coffee and sat at the secretary's desk to go over the notes she had made. She was not unorganized, but whatever way she was organizing and communicating with Galloway was apparently not pleasing the man. Albert spent the remainder of his day doing his best to learn what system would work for the way Galloway worked. He soon discovered that Galloway was the unorganized one. Stacks of files and papers were haphazardly thrown across his desk and a large table in the corner. Several filing cabinets lined the wall of one room and a bookshelf full of law books. But the filing cabinets were barely sorted, and the only thing in the room that was in order was the books.

He decided that room would be his first project, and he would develop a system that he and the secretary could work on together. Between the two of them, Albert hoped that they would be able to keep Galloway's files squared away. Albert wondered how a man who was so outwardly disarrayed could be so incredibly successful.

Albert was less surprised as the day went on that Galloway had so carelessly offered him an apprenticeship two years prior and proceeded to forget about it. When he took the third cup of coffee to the man, he caught sight of the dozens of notes. It seemed that the older man could not remember a single thing unless it was written down and posted in front of him. Albert learned to keep detailed notes each time the phone rang and realized that his job here may be more important than the old man cared to admit. Clearly, something was not right in his head.

It would take a while, Albert decided, to find his footing. But if he was good at anything, it was adjusting to new circumstances and information. Change bothered him little. It kept life interesting and enjoyable.

He had little time to think over the investigation of Rebecca's mother since he had seen her two days prior. How could he think about the past and investigations when he was so caught up in Rebecca? She had been the girl of his dreams for most of his childhood and all of his adolescence. Though he had never breathed a word of it to a single soul, nor hinted at his feelings in any way, they had always been there. When he had gone off to college, he had begun to put it behind him, realizing what was obvious: she was meant to marry John Templeton. He had put it so far behind him, in fact, that other than wanting the best for her, he had not allowed himself to consider the possibility that she was free or available when her engagement had fallen apart. It was not until the ball the other night, and then again when she had clung to his arm in front of John, that Albert had felt those old feelings awaken within him again.

Now his thoughts were circling around her. Her beauty. The softness of her voice. Her ability to speak her mind, to confidently know her thoughts, and yet never speak more than needed to be said. She had a humility about her that he had never before known in her. He supposed it was the falling from her renowned societal place to where she was now. She no longer behaved or held herself as an heiress who had never seen hardship or embarrassment.

When her worst moment in life—her confrontation of John and the dissolution of their engagement had taken place so publicly—he wondered what had really changed in her. For the first time, he regretted being absent for that episode of her life. Now she was rebuilt and new. And he would have to rediscover who she was.

The front office door opened, and a young mail carrier stepped in, shaking the rain from his coat. He was already digging through his bag as he stepped toward Albert at the desk and made quick work of handing the mail to him. After Albert handed him a stack of outgoing mail, he trotted back out the door.

Albert anxiously reached for the letter opener and ripped into an express letter he had been waiting on.

*Albert,*

*I received your express. It's good to hear from you. Let's catch up soon. As far as Mrs. Bedford's medical records, you know I am not allowed to disclose those. You ask quite a lot of me, and I am sure you will now be in my debt.*

The note was from Clarisse, who had been two years his junior in school and he had tutored her in her history classes. Now she was an assistant at the hospital, studying to be a nurse. Albert had written her, hoping to cash in a favor by asking for Hannah Bedford's medical records. If his suspicions were correct, the powder in the envelope was arsenic. He hoped beyond hope that it had been prescribed to Mrs. Bedford as a treatment for her ailments, and not that he was dealing with something far worse.

*Mrs. Bedford, it appears was diagnosed with nothing more than headaches and hypochondria. It seems there was nothing much wrong with her at all, but Dr. Dickson and Dr. Hartford were called to the Bedford home several times a month. In her final months, there are records of Dr. Dickson seeing her two or three times a week. It seems he prescribed her nothing more than placebos. Her condition was completely mental and she must have died from malnutrition or something of the sort. I am sure her death records have been sealed, given the status of the family, and I see no cause of death recorded anywhere.*

The rest of the message went on with Clarisse renewing her desire to see him, and Albert folded the letter and tucked it away inside his suit pocket with a frown across his features. It had been widely circulated by the Bedford family that Mrs. Bedford suffered a heart condition. Apparently, that had been a falsehood, and Albert wondered who else besides Mrs. Bedford's doctors knew that. What about Rebecca? What did she know of her mother's death?

Her final medical records might be sealed, but he could at least find the record of her death at the church. He would be able to use the date to look up archived newspapers and read the obituary for himself. While he knew he could simply ask Rebecca, he did not want to unnecessarily alarm her. He was not supposed to be investigating deaths, after all. He was supposed to be investigating the mystery man.

Albert sighed. He would have to send word to Robert and Caroline not to hold dinner for him, not if he was going to breach the doors of St. Andrews for the first time in two years and explain his, the son of one of the most affluent and religiously devoted men in Victoria, absence from the Catholic faith.

"Albert!" Galloway's voice bellowed as the man's office door shot open.

He whirled around to face him. "Yes, sir?"

"*Carlill versus Carbolic Smoke Ball Co.* Do you know it?"

Albert searched his memory. "Yes, sir. The courts ruled in favor of Mrs. Carlill. Advertisements are legally binding between the company and the consumer."

Galloway nodded. "Very good. I need every bit of information you can find on it. Paul Bedford is going to sue Darhun Carriages. And he's requested you to sit in with me."

A massive lump formed in Albert's throat and he tried desperately to swallow it down.

"Paul Bedford, sir?"

"Yes, apparently he learned you are working for me now and wanted to see what you are made of."

*"Or he knows I was in his home with his daughter the same day she rejected John Templeton again,"* Albert thought.

Clarity dawned on him. Paul Bedford was a deep thinker. Albert hated to call him manipulative, but he had a way of getting what he wanted. It made him a successful, well-respected businessman. But it made him a person no one wanted to cross. It had once been Paul Bedford's greatest desire to unite his family with the Templeton family, and Albert seriously doubted John's youthful indiscretions had doused much of that desire.

Had Paul Bedford been the one who had arranged for John to come back to Victoria to once again ask for Rebecca's hand? Albert hated how much he suspected that it had been. If the man had been informed by either John or the loyal butler that Albert had interrupted that conversation, Albert would need to be careful. One did not cross Paul Bedford without feeling ramifications.

It was going to be a long night of sorting through all his thoughts concerning the Bedford family.

Rebecca received Albert in the parlor with a look of great anticipation. He allowed himself to believe for the whole of a second that it was simply his presence she had looked forward to. But he knew that in reality, she was likely caught up in the feeling of excitement that came with searching for clues and answers to big questions. Unfortunately, he had no answers she really wanted. He was no closer to identifying the man in the picture or the diaries. He had returned home the night before from his visit to St. Andrews, having survived a harrowing conversation with the rector of the church where he admitted he had converted to Protestantism. He felt no shame in admitting it, but he hated the look of disappointment on the face of the man who had guided the religious faith of the Harrington family since Albert was born.

Coming from that conversation, he had not been prepared for the explicit details Hannah Bedford had written of her relationship with her lover. He blushed scarlet, his mouth going dry, each time he recalled the words. In fact, while the enormous portrait of the elegant and socially distinguished Hannah Bedford hanging above the mantlepiece had always struck him as a great likeness to the actual lady, he now saw it in a whole new light. So much more made up that woman than what she ever allowed to meet the eye.

His eyes drifted from the image of the mother to the beautiful daughter standing before him. Their auburn locks shined in the same hue, their pale skin both seemingly flawless, except for the single freckle just to the right of Rebecca's nose. Their facial structure was different in small ways, such as the slight crookedness to Rebecca's nose where he knew Henry had broken it with a lacrosse stick when they were young, and Rebecca had the most striking green eyes he had ever seen, where according to the portrait above him, her mother's eyes were brown.

And above all, Rebecca had an air of purity and innocence about her. Albert suspected, given the state of scandalous affairs surrounding her, that he might be the only one to think so. But in his eyes, she practically glowed, casting a joy into his heart that he only knew in her presence. He hated the thought of her reading her mother's diaries at that moment. Hated that the vision she had once had of her mother was going to be forever changed by this hunt they were on.

"Good afternoon, Rebecca," Albert greeted her.

He was quick and to the point but watched her reaction with care. It was clear that she had no idea her mother had not truly been ill. She pressed a hand to her chest, brows knit together in confusion.

"But then how? Why? Why did she die?" Rebecca asked bravely.

Albert put a hand to her shoulder, gauging her reaction to that as well. She either did not notice or was not disturbed by it. "I do not know the answer to that yet, Rebecca. But I will do my best to find out."

"Please...whatever it is. Promise me you will not go to authorities without asking me first."

"Do you suspect foul play?" Albert asked, not hiding the shock from his face.

"Don't you?" she fired back.

At the sound of the front door opening and male voices in the entryway, Rebecca froze, eyes growing wide. "My father is home," she whispered.

Uncertainty washed over him. He knew the implication of being seen here, calling on Rebecca, by none other than her father. And he had done so without first seeking permission, which was a highly dishonorable thing to do. He reminded himself that it was not really like that. He was not courting Rebecca. She had hired him to do a job; though it was a job about which he could tell no one, especially her father. Meaning that exactly what this situation was not, was exactly what it would look like, and he had no other explanation to give.

"Rebecca?" her father called, leading her to wince.

"Yes? I'm in the parlor!" she called back, and they heard his footsteps before they saw him.

He was just as Albert remembered him, though his hair and mustache were almost completely peppered with gray. His round reading glasses were pushed to the end of his nose as they always were. His pinstripe sack suit was gray too, and his hands were in his pockets. His green eyes immediately ran up and down Albert's length.

"Entertaining men unaccompanied are we, Rebecca?" he asked, his eyes never leaving Albert's face. They were locked in a stare down, and Albert knew that if he looked away first, he would win nothing but the title of coward.

"Just an old friend, Father," Rebecca said. "I'm sure you remember him. This is—"

"Albert Harrington," Paul Bedford cut his daughter off as he rocked on his feet. "Yes, I know exactly who he is. I also know this is his second visit to my home and to my daughter without asking for permission to see you."

"Edwin…" Rebecca muttered under her breath.

"Yes, Edwin. He's loyal to me, Rebecca darling.

And to you. He knows it is not in your best interest to have a man visiting you without my consent. Let's face the facts, your reputation cannot take another blow."

Albert's fist curled at his side as Rebecca's face flushed scarlet. He could not help it. He could not stand the idea of anyone embarrassing or hurting her.

"Father," Rebecca begged, and Albert remembered her telling him what she believed her father thought of her. Just a means to an end. A pawn with which to gain financially and socially.

"And what of your reputation, Albert?" Paul Bedford turned his sharp eyes back to him. Albert was ashamed to feel himself cower even an inch under the gaze. His mind flashed to Robert, of his business dealings, his desire to work with Paul Bedford in the future. Albert knew he needed to tread carefully. To lose the respect of this man, or even to for a moment take his actions too lightly would be detrimental to the future of the Harrington name. "Why do you sneak behind my back?"

"That was not my intention. I simply—" Albert felt his hands beginning to sweat. He thought of his niece, swallowing hard to find the words he needed to assure this man of his own respectability.

"Yes, I am sure it was not," he interrupted, and Albert searched his tone, wondering if he was sincere or sarcastic. "Well, Albert, knowing who you are, the reputation of your family, your level of education, and so forth, I heartily give my consent to your courting my daughter. Though let's keep the door open and have Alice in here with you, for propriety's sake."

Albert blinked, the conversation having had taken a hard and fast turn. He was sure not to let his jaw drop, though it desperately wanted to.

"Father! He did not ask you," Rebecca screeched. "And quite frankly, sir, I am well past the age of needing you to approve who I see."

"Hush, Rebecca," he chided impatiently as he turned to head back out the door. "You received what you wanted. Must you ruin it by arguing?"

Her mouth clamped shut, but Albert saw her cross her arms and tap her foot anxiously on the ground.

"You will receive an invitation to have dinner with the family soon, Albert," the older man called over his shoulder. "I will see you then."

"Yes, sir," Albert called after his retreating form. "Thank you, sir."

"Oh!" Rebecca moaned, plopping to the sofa with her arms still folded over her chest like a little girl throwing a tantrum. "He is impossible. I am so sorry, Albert."

He shrugged, feeling some sort of elation rising up in him as he sat next to her. Paul Bedford approved Albert Harrington of seeing his daughter? Perhaps he truly had given up hope of seeing Rebecca matched with an heir of great fortune. Albert was not poor by any means, but he would have a career outside the family business, and it was Robert who had inherited the mass of the family fortune, properties, and business.

"Do not apologize. At least now we can continue the investigation without so much sneaking around. This will be helpful."

"You don't see it, do you? He manipulated the situation in his favor. He is right. I cannot withstand another failed relationship. He will spread the news of this like wildfire, and as soon as they," she gestured wildly toward the window, but he knew she meant the entire city of Victoria, "hear of it, you and I will have no choice but to marry."

"Would that truly be so terrible?" he asked softly, as if he was afraid of waking a bear.

"Yes," she nodded, though she seemed less than certain. "I do not wish to marry. I do not think I am suited for it, the expectations, the looking past faults of the other person... and I do not really have to marry. I am my father's heiress. And after my father dies, I will still have Henry to stand for me as needed. I will never have a want in the world. Why would I want to give up my freedom?"

"Marriage is not a prison, Rebecca," Albert argued, knowing he was speaking against years of bitterness in her heart.

She shook her head, placing her hands over his. "Please, my dear friend, let's not talk about this anymore."

Albert felt the temptations of defeat looming at the edges of his mind, but he would not let them win. He believed God could redeem what John had damaged. He would continue this battle another day.

"I should go," Albert stood. "My brother and sister-in-law will be expecting me. I will continue looking into everything we discussed. Goodbye."

He left quickly, hearing her squeak out a surprised goodbye at his sudden retreat. Edwin opened the door for him and handed him his hat, which Albert promptly placed on his head before stepping out into the warm sun. He let out a breath of air and squared his shoulders, knowing he would mull over that conversation for the entire trip home, and hoping desperately for the distraction of playing with his niece when he arrived at Harrington House.

Rebecca stared at the seat Albert had vacated for a long moment. The afternoon had taken a surprising turn, her father having swooped in to control her life once more. She desperately wished he had gone on pretending she did not exist. But the man was never one to miss an opportunity. She had ruined his plans for her future once before, and he had punished her for it for too long. She had enough.

She was about to rise to storm after him and let him know just how she felt about what he had just done, but she stopped in her tracks. There was no way to explain Albert's presence if she denied that they had an interest in courting. Her father would demand that Albert stop visiting and ruining her chances of securing another young man. That would be the end of the investigation she had spent so many hours obsessing over.

Rebecca needed to know the truth about her mother more than she needed almost anything. It was the only way she would be able to sleep at night. It was one thing living in this house with a father who was so openly disappointed in everything she did. But she could not live with the thought that her mother would be disappointed in her too if she knew the mess Rebecca had created. The woman had spent all of her years raising her, attempting to iron out the stubborn pride that had made Rebecca so unable to forgive John in the first place.

The thought that her perfect mother had an imperfect past had started her on this journey. It had bridged the wide gap Rebecca felt existed between her own character and the character of her mother. She wanted to hear her father's comparisons of them and for once in her life to know that he was wrong. But now, knowing that there was more to the story, that her mother's death was suspicious, Rebecca had opened a jar she could never close. Having Albert around was the only way to find out what had happened and who in this house she needed to mistrust.

There was no choice. She would have to allow her father to think she was courting Albert to continue the investigation. She collapsed back against the sofa with an unladylike growl, knowing her father was somewhere in that house with a smug look on his face thinking he had won.

## CHAPTER 7

*R*ebecca did not see Albert again until Friday. She was surprised to discover how much she was anxiously awaiting his return. She did not doubt that Albert would keep his commitment to help her, but she was concerned that he would be less willing after her father's behavior. Albert had been rudely reminded of how much damage helping her could cause to him.

She knew Albert had been sweet on her when they were younger. He had turned red anytime she looked at him. But that had not been unlike the reaction she had received from any of the men her age. However, those looks had vanished the moment she had rejected John. Albert had not been in Victoria for any of that, and she had the advantage of his ignorance at first. Now that her father had so blatantly reminded him of it right in front of her, she felt the crushing weight of fear that she would now be rejected by him too. She would not deny that having Albert turn away from her as the rest of them had would hurt deeply.

On Thursday, however, much to her relief, he sent her a note asking if there was any other place in the house that her mother might have stored heirlooms, letters, or mementos from her life in England. There was, of course, the attic. But she had not ventured up there in years. As a little girl, she had been nearly frightened to death by the shadows and eerie sounds that could be heard from that poorly lit, cobweb-filled place. She had suffered nightmares for days, and when she finally confessed to her mother what had frightened her, her adventure to the unknown land of that upper room, her mother forbade her from going up there again.

Although now, as she pondered Albert's note and wondered what sort of things her mother may have hidden up there, she wondered if her mother had forbidden her from going up there because she was afraid of what Rebecca might find. She was filled with a fresh sense of guilt. What had changed in her to suddenly question the motives of her beloved mother?

She wondered if she was pursuing the right

course of action, or if she simply should have let the past rest in peace. Hannah Bedford had been the epitome of what every woman in their society should strive to be; all kindness, duty-centered, focused on hospitality and charity, a pillar in the work and worship at St. Andrews, and so forth. She had been highly regarded and respected by all. And Rebecca was expected to carry on that legacy in word and deed.

And she had. Until John Templeton had an affair and Rebecca had decided she was worthy of more than to make such a great personal sacrifice of her own heart and happiness so that others could be pleased with her. That Rebecca Bedford—who had confronted John in a room full of people, certain that others would take her side, who had turned down that offer of marriage and naively believed that her father would support her decision to walk away from such a man—had been rudely awakened.

They wanted her to stay silent. They wanted her to be a replica of her mother. They wanted her to turn a blind eye and marry John Templeton because it was expected. Because it would have united the two most wealthy and powerful families in Victoria. And she had failed them.

She had told herself it did not matter. She could live with their disapproval as long as she did not have to spend her nights with a man she deplored. But as time had gone on, she had instead begun to spend her nights sweating in the guilt of wondering if her mother was disappointed in her too. If her mother had been alive at the time of the incident, would her mother have demanded she set aside her desires to be valued in order to appease society? She had never once seen her mother go against her father. She likely would not have then either, unless she was capable of understanding the deep hurt she was feeling.

So that first day of uncovering her mother's past had felt like a step toward reconciling within herself the fact that her mother would have sided with her. If her mother had known the pain of society pulling her away from being loved and into a marriage she had not originally wanted, she would have stopped at nothing to protect her daughter from such pain. Rebecca had felt closer to her then.

But now, as the investigation seemed to be raising more questions and uncertainty, she felt a chasm opening up between her and her deceased mother once more. Where would she draw the line? How much truth would be too much, burying her in pain that she could not face?

Rebecca knew there were likely secrets to uncover in the attic, but she dared not go there. Not alone. She was afraid of what she would find and afraid to face it alone. So she waited until Friday when Albert came, determined to make him go with her. What she did not expect was the pale and dread-filled look on his face when he entered the house that Friday afternoon.

"What is it?" She asked immediately after the expected greetings.

He did not answer immediately. Instead, his eyes turned to Alice. Her lady's maid sat in a chair in the corner of the room reading a book. She was present per her father's request, though the whole idea was very annoying to Rebecca. Her presence meant that she and Albert would have a much more difficult time discussing the investigation. If the household staff were to catch wind, the gossip would be uncontrollable. The whole of Victoria would know about it by noon the next day.

"This is Alice," Rebecca told him. "My lady's maid."

Clearly, he wanted nothing to do with talking in front of her. He motioned for her to join him further across the room.

In a hushed voice he said, "I've discovered an alarming truth. The powder was what I feared."

"In the envelope?" she clarified.

Albert nodded. "Arsenic."

"Well, surely the doctors must have prescribed it for her ailments."

"Non-existent ailments, Rebecca. And no, I have been over her medical records three times, as has the nurse whom I originally contacted. There is no prescription of arsenic anywhere."

Rebecca swallowed and turned to the other woman in the room. "Alice, will you go see about having a tray of tea prepared, please?"

"But—" the young girl tried to argue.

"Please," Rebecca's tone was not unkind, but it was firm. She watched the woman scurry out of the room. When she was gone, she turned back to Albert. "Albert, speak plainly to me. What does this mean?"

"It could mean multiple things," Albert told her. "One, that your mother realized she was not being given real medicine. I noticed that her care shifted from Dr. Harford to Dr. Dickson in her final months."

Rebecca remembered it well. Her mother shrieking at Dr. Harford one morning when he had been called to the home, and Father flying up the stairs to her room, demanding that her care be handled by someone else from that point on.

"She may have decided to treat herself and given herself doses of arsenic. It is not all that hard to obtain on ones' own, so she could have done so. It would have poisoned her over time."

"Why would she do such a thing?"

"I have no idea. The other option, of course, is far worse."

"Someone did it to her," Rebecca felt instantly nauseous.

"I find that highly unlikely, given that there does not seem to be a motive. Did you uncover anything else here?"

Rebecca shook her head, explaining to him her hesitancy to approach the attic on her own. Alice had not yet returned with the tea tray, so they took the opportunity to head upstairs. The door to the attic was at the end of a hall, just past the glass-paned double doors that opened into the library. Rebecca gave it a firm tug when it refused to budge, and it responded by flinging rapidly open. She stumbled back, landing against Albert's chest. His hands were immediately on her shoulders to steady her. Her heart fluttered at the contact and she turned her head to see him blushing as always.

"Sorry," she apologized, but he was already reaching around her for the light switch.

The lights over the stairs were dim, and she moved to let Albert pass her first, and then followed him up. When she reached the top, they both stood in the center of the room surveying the area. Boxes of all shapes and sizes, old pieces of furniture, trunks and old paintings. It was drafty and creaky, and she unconsciously stepped closer to Albert for protection.

"This could take hours to sort through," Albert groaned. "Does anything stand out to you specifically as your mother's?"

"Shouldn't we be looking for things that don't stand out? Things that are hidden?" she questioned.

Albert grinned at her, and she was powerless to keep from smiling back. "All right. I can agree with that. Let's each take a half of the room. Keep an eye out for old letters, photographs, anything from her childhood home."

Rebecca agreed, knowing exactly where she would start as they split up. The trunk filled with her mother's old clothes. She knew that it was where her mother's wedding dress was stored, and Rebecca had been told to never touch it. Her mother promised to show it to her when the time was right, but not a moment before. Rebecca had always respected this rule, enjoying the mystery and magic of knowing one day the dress would be pulled out for her wedding day. Now, however, as she did everything these days, Rebecca wondered what else was in the trunk.

"Here's a box of old letters from your grandparents," Albert called from across the room. Rebecca turned to look at him, her breath hitching in her throat as she took in his image, concentrating so fully on the papers in front of him. His broad shoulders filled out his white collared shirt, his suit jacket discarded over the back of a dusty chair. His dark hair looked freshly cut, she noticed, and she found herself wanting to run her fingers through it.

Rebecca shook the cobwebs from her brain, chided herself for allowing herself to let her father's schemes work their way into her mind, and busied herself with prying open the trunk that had not been opened in probably a decade.

The top gave way and she pushed it open with a loud creak. The smell of age and undisturbed air billowed out to her, and tears filled her eyes as a fresh moment of grief washed over her. Folded neatly and carefully wrapped in tissue, on top of the trunk full of her mother's most precious mementos, was the wedding dress. Her fingers timidly unfolded the tissue until her eyes finally rested on the beautiful white lace of the bodice. She hesitated to touch it, and as soon as she did, the tears spilled. She dared not lift it out and look at the entire thing, knowing she would disintegrate into a pile of sobs, wanting her mother so desperately. She needed to focus on the task at hand.

After wrapping the dress back up, she pulled the bundle out and set it on an old rocking chair. Then she turned back to the trunk. A soft smile mixed with her tears as she found things that her mother had kept from her childhood and adolescence, things she had found important enough to bring with her from England.

There was a light pink box in the far-left corner, the lid tied shut with a white ribbon. Rebecca knelt down in front of the trunk and reached for it, remembering how she had done so at the age of eight to have her mother quickly swat her hand away. It was the last time Mother had ever spoken to Rebecca about England, or her maternal grandparents, the last time she had opened the trunk to share any memories with her daughter.

Now Rebecca's heart pounded wildly, half expecting her mother to appear over her and scold her once more. But only the sound of Albert riffling through papers filled her ears. She lifted the box and placed it in her lap. Slowly, she lifted the lid to find the box full of baby items. A single white bootie, a rattle, a lock of blonde hair tied up with string, and a picture of a baby in a Christening gown, held in the arms of an unknown woman and surrounded by two men. Rebecca's heart stopped. The man on the left… she held the picture closer … yes, it was him. The man in the journals. Rebecca felt her mouth go dry as she flipped the picture over. Scribbled on the back she read, *Christening, Helena Mercier, 10 January 1887. She's beautiful, my love.*

Who was this child? Rebecca both questioned and knew the answer at the same time. It was all adding up in her mind; she knew she was letting her thoughts run ahead of the evidence, but it seemed so obvious now. The passionate love affair with this man, the missing year, and her parents shipping her off as far as possible to Victoria, Canada to marry a man who would be none the wiser to his young wife's past until it was too late.

She was shaking. Her breath was shallow. But she needed the confirmation, the final puzzle piece to this mystery, and she knew she had laid eyes on it at the bottom of the box. A birth record, or rather, what looked to be a duplicate of one, for it lacked an official seal of any kind. Rebecca removed a small, child-size ballet slipper from the box and then pulled out the paper and braced herself for what was to come.

*Baby girl Helena Mary Alice Mercier born 2 January 1887*

*Surrendered at time of birth, Witness: Abigail Adams and Antoine Alexander Mercier*

*Mother: Anonymous, Father: Andre Alexander Mercier*

Her gasp for air was loud and sudden, and she dropped the paper into the box like it had burned her. Albert was immediately at her side, reaching for the items in her lap, talking to her but sounding as if he was far away. Blood was rushing in her ears and she could not focus enough to hear him.

This was the result of her mother's premarital love affair. She had become pregnant, been sent away to give birth to the child, and immediately been forced to give the child away to the father's family. Rebecca had opened Pandora's box, and wanted so desperately to shove it all back inside, far away, and to never learn a bit of it.

She had a sister. Somewhere, out there in the world, was a sister who likely had no idea what had truly happened to her mother or who she had been. And Andre? Did he live still? Rebecca felt every memory of her relationship with her mother, her own parents' actions over the years replay in her mind in a whole new perspective.

Albert had rifled through enough of the things in the box to piece it together, and he reached for her. She was shaking uncontrollably, and his arms folded around her as he knelt next to her on the floor. She had expected the love affair. But a child out of wedlock? It was the reason for the missing year of her mother's diaries. If she had ever dared to write about the events surrounding that scandal, she had likely had the sense to destroy them.

In the safety of Albert's arms, she began to calm. Her heart longed for her mother in that moment more than it had in a long time. Only this time it was because Rebecca wanted to offer her comfort. The pain she must have endured, entirely on her own, forced to give her daughter away and never see her again. The items in the box were daring and risky mementos of that child's existence, but Rebecca figured her mother had been desperate to keep anything she could.

"Rebecca…" Albert waved a hand in front of her face and she snapped back with another gasp. "Rebecca, your maid… she's calling for us. We must go downstairs. You must pull yourself together. You cannot let on what you have learned, not for anything in the world, until we decide what to do. Do you understand?"

Rebecca nodded mutely, watching as Albert tucked everything back into the trunk and sealed it once more. Everything but the birth record and the picture, which he tucked into his pocket. Then he reached for her hand and pulled her down the attic stairs.

"Miss Bedford!"

Rebecca heard her maid's panicked voice searching for her somewhere in the house.

"Here, Alice!" Rebecca called back, and saw the woman appear at the bottom of the main flight of stairs. They made their way toward her, meeting her at the bottom.

"Oh, Miss Rebecca, your tea… it has been ready several minutes. It will get cold."

She saw the way the woman glanced at Albert, and then at her. Rebecca realized how the situation looked. It looked worse when Albert realized his jacket was still upstairs and went back up for it. Alone in the hallway with her lady's maid, Rebecca sought to dissuade her from the scandalous conclusions she was likely coming to.

"We were in the attic looking for father's old maps. Do you know where they are, Alice? I wanted to show them to Albert."

"Yes, Miss, they are in the library. You and Master Henry were looking at them not a week ago," Alice gave her a look that told Rebecca she saw straight through her fib. "But you should have waited for me anyway, and I would have looked with you. That is my kind of job, Miss Rebecca."

"Oh, we were quite all right," Rebecca reached for Alice's hand and stepped very close to her, voice and grip firm. "You will say nothing of this to anyone, do you understand?"

Alice nodded frantically, and both women looked over to Albert who had returned and fixed Alice with a hard glare. Alice recoiled and stepped aside to let them pass back into the parlor. Rebecca settled into the sofa and Albert knelt in front of her.

"Rebecca, are you well?" Albert asked.

"What will I do?" she whispered, tears pouring down her face. "My mother had a child out of wedlock and that information could ruin the family forever."

"Yes," he nodded. "You knew that when we started."

"But… " she trailed off.

"This is not what you expected. I know." His face was full of sympathy. Timidly, his hand reached up to her cheek, wiping away an unwanted tear.

"We can stop the investigation, get rid of the evidence. But… there is still more to learn. How did your mother die, Rebecca? Do you still want to know? Can you face that truth, whatever it is?"

"I… I… " she stammered. "Oh, Albert. I need time. I need to think. Father will be home any minute. You should go. Come back tomorrow?"

He nodded, studying her for a moment more, and then he stood to his feet. "I will look further into this. Try to provide more clarity."

She nodded, not able to respond. When he had reached the door, he turned back.

"Rebecca," he said, and she turned to look at him. Their eyes met, and her heart lurched under the intensity of his gaze. "People make mistakes. Do not hold this against her. She was very young… and in love."

The words stung, but not because they were said about her mother. She knew the irony of the situation, the hypocrisy she would live in if she forgave her mother for this massive transgression covered up with lies but refused to forgive John for the same thing. She turned away from Albert. She heard the door open and close, and then she hurried to her bedroom and closed the door, dissolving into a pile of sobs on the rug.

Albert placed his hat firmly on his head and stepped out into the sun with a heavy sigh. He knew his words had hurt her, he had seen the pain flicker across her face. He knew why. He had his own bitterness to wrestle with when it came to John Templeton.

He had not been as shocked by the discovery as Rebecca had. He had half expected a child born out of wedlock to be the case the moment he had riffled through Hannah Bedford's diaries. What he had not expected was a box full of mementos of the occasion. He wondered how the woman had dared to keep them in that house where her husband could so easily find them. Albert did not want to be one to jump to outlandish conclusions but knowing what he did about Paul Alexander Bedford's desire to maintain social status, he could not help himself. If he was so willing to toss aside his daughter's happiness and wish her to marry a man who had broken her heart, what would stop him from reacting poorly to discovering his wife was in love with someone else and had a secret child?

To Albert, the question was just how poorly he would react to such a truth. Enough to have his wife slowly poisoned? If that was the case, Albert wanted to move quickly to wrap up the loose ends of the mystery. If Rebecca was in danger, Albert planned to get her out of that house as soon as possible.

## CHAPTER 8

*A*lbert looked up from where he was bent over his desk, mid-bite into an apple, as the office door swung open.

"Mr. Bedford!" Albert exclaimed, jumping to his feet. "What can I do for you, sir?"

"I was in the area and hoped to speak with Ernest about my case. He would not happen to be available would he?"

"He is," Albert nodded. "Allow me to tell him you are here." Albert turned to head toward Galloway's office, but Mr. Bedford cleared his throat in the way one only does when they have something more to say. Albert's feet slowed, his heart pounding.

"Mr. Harrington..."

"Call me Albert, please," Albert turned toward

him with a smile. "Or I'll always be looking over my shoulder for my brother."

Paul Bedford's eyes crinkled in amusement. Albert noticed the lines there, built up from years of smiling and laughing. It surprised Albert, for though he had not seen much of the always working man when he was young and running in circles with the man's children, he had never known him to be an overly kind or joyful man. Especially not since the death of his wife.

"Albert," Mr. Bedford nodded, pushing his hands into his pockets. "I understand you were in my attic with my daughter the other day."

Albert was certain the world had tipped, and he felt the blood rush out of his face. Did he know? Did he know what Albert and Rebecca were up to? Or did he suspect Albert was disrespecting his daughter?

But Mr. Bedford just laughed. "It has made me very happy to see you spending time with my daughter. I am sure you know that she has not been the interest of anyone, except as a topic of gossip, since that nasty business with John Templeton."

Albert did not like the way in which he spoke, his tone making it seem as though Rebecca was in the wrong.

"It surprised me, when Edwin first told me you

had called. He told me of the tumultuous disagreement between Mr. Templeton and Rebecca and about how you interrupted the whole thing. Imagine my shock to learn from my butler that my daughter had announced her relationship with you to John before she announced it to me. Now, under normal circumstances, I would feel disrespected, furious even, and expect you to apologize for courting my daughter behind my back. But things with Rebecca have been difficult at best as of late, and I simply feel thankful to find some small hope that my daughter may not remain unmarried her whole life."

He looked like a catfish, he was sure, his mouth popping open and closed as he stammered desperately without a single word coming to mind in how to reply to such a speech. But apparently, he was not expected to say anything at all, as Mr. Bedford continued to have the whole conversation himself.

"I say all this so you will know that there is no disagreement or conceit between us, Albert. I heartily give my consent. In fact, I have made reservations for you tonight at the finest establishment in town. I've told Rebecca you will pick her up at seven sharp. I expect you to have her home no later than nine. And, beyond that, I would like you to consider this a formal invitation to family dinner on Sunday. Rebecca can fill you in on the details tonight."

"Uh, I do not know what to say," Albert finally strung a few words together. "Thank you, sir. But I do want you to know that I can secure my own dates with your daughter from here on."

"Good. I would expect no less. I will just say, I am eager for you two to make it publicly official. Now, that's settled, would you please tell Ernest I am here?"

Albert turned to find Galloway already opening his office door. "Paul! I thought I heard you. Come on in."

The two men disappeared into the office and closed the door firmly behind them. Albert moved in a fog, back toward his desk. He knew he looked like he had seen a ghost, and he felt a bit like it too. Never in his life had he felt so controlled or manipulated. He was ashamed he had not stood up for himself. And yet, if he were truly honest, down to the bottom of his soul, he would have to admit that he had not fought back or argued because in the end, he was getting the result he wanted. He was taking Rebecca Bedford out to dinner.

He was determined to enjoy it, determined not to let his eyes wander to the people who would see them out together that evening and begin to gossip as Mr. Bedford so clearly hoped they would. Half of Victoria would know Albert was courting Rebecca by tomorrow. He tried not to think about what that could mean for the rest of the Harrington family if he tied them to a woman entrenched in stains of the past. Instead, he prayed they could look past them as he was.

Rebecca had allowed her worst side to come out that day. She had behaved like a young and immature girl the moment her father had told her of the plans he had made for her that evening. How dare he, she had questioned, wondering aloud how long he planned to control her and treat her like a child. He had responded that he would treat her like a child for as long as she acted like one. He hurled insults at her, telling her it was her refusal to submit herself as a woman should that required him to step in and take over.

Matters had been made worse when she had looked to Henry for support but, ever the obedient son, he had ducked out of the house mumbling something about taking Anne for a drive. Just before he had made his escape, she had thrown another tantrum about his interest in Anne. Her father had sent her to her room and told her not to come down until Albert arrived.

After she had calmed down and Alice had begun preparing her for the evening, she was filled with shame. If Albert had seen her behave that way, she was certain he would never step foot in the house again. She was entirely undeserving of his kindness or his good faith.

Truthfully, she was glad to be spending time with him. Never before had she felt as whole as she did when in his presence. He saw her. He cared about her, and not for what she could offer him financially, but for her person. Though she had clearly hidden parts of herself from him, she knew Albert would be there for her even if she wore sacks and had not a penny to her name.

Albert was different from any of the others. He was truly good, deep down in his soul. It was a wonder to her that he had grown up in this same society she had, and yet ended up so incredibly kind and tenderhearted. She had felt free to allow him to be there for her over the past weeks, as she had never allowed anyone else to be.

No, spending time with him was not the problem. It was the way her father had manipulated the situation to his own advantage. He would trap Albert into marrying her if it was the last thing he did, and Rebecca knew if he was successful in doing so, it would ruin it for her. Albert would resent her, as she would cause damage to his reputation as she carried with her all the scandal she did.

She determined to enjoy the evening with him as much as she possibly could, enjoy being truly seen and the feeling of worth that he gave her, knowing she would need to walk away from him before they reached the point of no return.

Albert arrived at the Bedford's front door and was ushered into the parlor where Paul Bedford sat, newspaper in hand and right foot resting on his left knee.

"Albert…" The older man stood and extended a hand. "Right on time, I see."

"Yes, sir," Albert nodded, a curious case of butter-flies in his stomach. He realized he had spent the last few hours building this evening up in his head. Or the last few years, if he were honest. In reality, Paul Bedford was pulling all of the strings, and this dinner was nothing more on Rebecca's part than a desire to hide what was really going on: the inves-tigation.

"Rebecca will be down in a few minutes. Please take a seat," Paul motioned to a chair, and Albert dutifully sat in it while Paul resumed his chair. "So tell me, Albert. What are your intentions with my daughter?"

"Father, please," Rebecca begged through gritted teeth from the open doorway, her tone flat.

Albert immediately stood to his feet and turned to find her wearing the same blue dress she had worn to the Whitlow's the first evening he had seen her again. The same dress that had taken his breath away. Now, as she had then, she looked uncomfortable with the situation, and perhaps even annoyed. She was here merely because her father required it of her. It was a sobering realization for Albert.

Paul Bedford chuckled. "She's just like her mother."

Albert's eyes flew to Rebecca's face and he watched her avert her eyes to the ground.

"You look lovely," Albert told her, drawing her attention back to him. "Shall we go?"

"Yes," Rebecca nodded, and then cast a cold glance to her father. "Anyone in particular you would like us to make sure sees us out together?"

Paul Bedford stood, face red with anger at her sarcastic tone. "I do not like what you are insinuating, Rebecca Elizabeth."

She shrugged, feigning innocence. "Just a simple question. We will see you later this evening, Father."

With that, she took Albert's hand and practically

yanked off his arm dragging him out the door. She was quiet the entire way to dinner, other than muttering about her irritation with her father. Albert tried to be patient and let her get past the conflict with her father, but he was desperate to know she was not irritated at him. Was she bothered to be going to dinner with him?

It was not until they were seated at the table, which was covered with fine china and white linens, that she began talking with him. She asked about his work, his time at Dalhousie, his family, and more. He filled her in on his desire to one day work in business and trade law. There was much need in a world that was growing ever smaller. She seemed genuinely interested in hearing more about it, asking questions that surprised him. It was evident she was well educated, and she knew more about her father's work than was expected. She left little room for him to ask questions the other way, until at last, he got an opening.

"Tell me about your life since I left. Since… well, you know."

"Since my engagement fell apart?" she looked wistfully toward the window. "My life is very small."

Albert heard the tone of boredom, of depression. He had a sudden urge to take her by the hand and pull her right out the door. Out of Victoria. Out of

British Columbia. He wanted to show her just how big the world was outside of her view. Instead, he settled for resting his hand over hers on the table. Their eyes met, and he was lost in a sea of sparkling green.

"I want to do so many things, but the ladies do their best to shove me out. The last charity fundraiser I tried to participate in, they gave me the smallest, most insignificant jobs they could. They are petty, and I cannot stand them."

"You know," Albert said, stabbing a boiled potato with his fork. "By locking yourself away in your home, you are giving them exactly what they want. You are a threat to them, Rebecca Bedford. At the end of the day, they know you did nothing wrong when it comes to John. And you are still the most beautiful woman out there. And, though I think it is a terrible reason to get married, you are still set to inherit. I know, and they know it too, that you are still very eligible for marriage."

Silence fell between them for a few moments, and when she spoke again, she changed the subject completely.

"So," Rebecca piped up over the candle, her face lit up by the light, her auburn hair framing her face with sweeping curls. "Henry was commenting to me how we have not seen you attending Mass with your family."

Albert swallowed, wiping his mouth with his napkin before he spoke. "No. No, I do not attend Mass any longer."

She looked up at him through her eyelashes, obviously trying to hide the concern from her face. The concern that he was a God-forsaken heathen. It was not the first time he had seen that look on someone's face.

"May I ask why?"

"Certainly," he smiled. "The most amazing thing happened while I was at Dalhousie, Rebecca. Truly remarkable. I found God… or rather, I believe He found me."

Rebecca slowly set down her fork, leaned back in her chair, and folded her hands in her lap. She looked entirely skeptical, confused, and maybe even a little irritated.

"I do not understand," she said flatly.

"Neither did I, at first," his smile widened. "I grew up… you and I both did… believing that God was a deity to please. Rules must be followed, ordinances practiced, church attended. Christian values must be visible in your life. You should always be ready to participate in acts of charity…"

"What's wrong with any of that?"

"Well... nothing in action, I suppose. But motives... for me my motivation was to please God and please others and get into heaven."

The blank look on her face he recognized well. He had had it on his face while sitting across the table from Edward Platt a year before, as with an open Bible, Edward had shared with Albert the true gospel.

"God revealed to me the truth of the matter. No matter how hard I work to please, I will never measure up to His goodness. I will never earn righteousness. Salvation is a work only He can do. I have opened my Bible and learned that salvation comes from faith, not works."

"You are Protestant," she said at length. Her tone did not hold the disdain he had expected, but it was not overly joyful at the realization either.

"I am a disciple of Christ."

"I have no idea what that means," Rebecca giggled awkwardly. "Forgive me, Albert, but I think you are..."

She trailed off. "Crazy?" he asked.

Rebecca looked terribly as if she did not want to admit it, but she nodded.

"Religion..." Albert went on to explain. "Religion is about guilt, I think. That was my experience. A set of rules to follow. Standards to live by. And always feeling as if you have fallen incredibly short. Do you disagree?"

Her head cocked to the side. "No."

"Take my father for example. He raised Robert and I to know without a doubt what was expected of us. The rules were clear. And Robert has dutifully followed them to the best of his ability. But I could not. I tried. I truly did. But I could not be what was expected of me. On my father's death bed, he finally acknowledged that, and he met me with grace. Loved me anyway. Told me I would always be his son, even if I could not meet those expectations. That was grace. And that is what God has done for us, Rebecca. Met us where we are, given us grace to believe in Him, to follow Him, and to forgive us when we fall short."

She looked down at her plate of food, and he could tell she had a lot going on in her mind. He decided not to push the issue further. It had taken him a long time to let go of his religious upbringing to begin a relationship with God built on faith instead of effort. Even after he had let go enough to pray with Edward to receive Christ, he had still struggled to let go of the desire to go to confession instead of praying directly to God himself. He had still desired to go to Mass, afraid that God would be disappointed or punish him. It had taken a lot for him to pick up the Bible and read it on his own. He had made a lot of progress toward believing in the gospel over the past year. He could not expect any different from her. He would give Rebecca time to digest it all.

"So I've heard that they added several wonderful desserts to the menu in my absence," Albert smiled at her, relieved when she returned it. "Any interest in those?"

Rebecca smiled at him, nodding eagerly, and Albert felt his heartbeat quicken as he realized once more that he was having dinner with the woman of his dreams. They walked home that evening, Rebecca happily on his arm, and took their time. He had the sense she did not want the evening to end. When they reached her block but were still out of sight of her house, she pulled him to a stop. He looked down at her, waiting on pins and needles to see what she would do, and she looked up at him, her head cocked softly to the side. She was standing so close, and their hands were intertwined between them.

He could not place a finger on her expression or identify what emotions were going on behind her eyes. She looked wishful and content and yet simultaneously melancholy. One of her hands freed itself from his grasp and she reached up, fingering the hair behind his ear. His breath stopped as they stared at one another. His head lowered, lips heading toward hers, and it seemed as if the moment he had waited half of his life for was about to happen. But she lowered her face at the last moment.

"Albert…" she whispered.

"I'm sorry," he rushed to apologize, but she shook her head.

"No. Do not apologize. Just… I cannot do this."

"I understand," he said softly.

"No, you don't," she looked back up with a sad smile, tears in her eyes.

Albert placed his lips to her forehead, certain that he did not, but willing himself to be patient with her in this as well. It seemed if he had waited this long, a while more would not kill him.

## CHAPTER 9

*R*ebecca was happy to admit dinner had gone well. She had dreaded the whole thing the moment her father had involved himself. She felt he had a tendency to rip the joy right out of things. Truthfully, if her father was going to assume she was courting anyone, she was glad it was Albert.

She knew eventually they would have to find a way to end this façade. And she also knew that at that point, another failed relationship under her belt, not a single soul would want to touch her. She would resign herself to be an "old maid" and to the continued vocal disappointment she endured from her father. Rebecca would make the most of her life as an unmarried woman. One day, when all the other ladies her age were settled in marriage and raising their children, they would leave Rebecca in peace to enjoy her life, to participate in charity work, and to pursue whatever other hobbies women were finding to amuse themselves. It would be a good life, as good as she could make it. And she would regret nothing, being happier single than in a relationship with a man she could not love or trust.

But now, after what she had to admit was a rather romantic and enjoyable evening with Albert, she was hesitant for it to end. After a moment on the sidewalk that she knew had ripped her heart in two, they made their way to the front door, and she smiled warmly at him to ease over any discomfort he had. Albert was expected to stay for a moment or two and share a conversation with her father, and she settled at the piano to fill the room with music. It was an end to a wonderful evening she had not spent thinking about her mother.

Albert settled with her father across the room, both of them enjoying a cigar and a drink. She heard them making small talk as she riffled through piano music. Once she had made her selection and sat down to play, she could no longer hear their conversation. They moved together toward the French doors that opened out to the garden, and leaving the doors open, they stepped outside into the night air. She assumed it was to allow the cigar smoke to have a place to escape and to enjoy the pleasant weather of the evening.

A light breeze made its way into the room, brushing hair across her face and playing at the edges of her sheet music. As she moved onto her third piece of music, she saw Albert and her father moving back into the room. Her father exited, leaving her alone with Albert, who slowly made his way toward her. He stood at her side, watching her play. Normally under such scrutiny, she would fumble over the keys, but with Albert she did not. He was like Henry. Kind, comforting, and free of a judging eye.

"May I speak with you?" Albert asked when she finished the piece.

Rebecca nodded, turning toward him on the piano bench.

"Your father and I were discussing my future plans," Albert mentioned. "Some of them I shared with you at dinner."

Rebecca nodded again. "I remember."

"But I have more plans…more dreams, that I have not spoken of yet. Not with you. I would like to now."

She swallowed, feeling a dread in her stomach. She had a strong suspicion of where this conversation was going, and if she was correct, Albert was going to force her to shove him away sooner than she wanted.

"Rebecca, I would like to tell you how much I have always admired you. Since we were very young… I've adored you, counted your acquaintance as a great treasure. Of course, you were always destined to be with John, and though I hated seeing the two of you together…"

"Albert," she sought to interrupt him, but he did not seem to hear her.

"I've begun to hope again, since I saw you at the Whitlow ball and gotten to know you once more, in a much more intimate way than I have ever been allowed before. You have changed in many ways, but I consider it all virtuous growth. My admiration for you has increased greatly."

"Albert," she said much more firmly as his hand reached for hers. "Please do not continue."

"I enjoy your friendship, Rebecca. But you must know I want us to be more than that."

"No. I told you I would not marry. John ruined that for me. I will not marry," she stood to her feet and moved away from him.

He frowned, clearly having not expected such a harsh reaction after what she had just allowed to happen outside. "I am not like him, Rebecca. I am not. Not in any way. And I think it is incredibly unfair of you to take away my chances, anyone's chances of winning your heart, because of him."

"I do not think I could trust you," Rebecca turned her tear-filled eyes away from him, offering him a view of her shoulder and the back of her head as he moved closer. It was not true. She trusted him with everything she had. But he was far too virtuous to walk away for the real reasons he should; she was certain she would ruin him and his family if the truth ever became known. It was far too much already to ask a man to look past her scandal with John. She knew he would argue with her, try to seek a way out for both of them. He would try to promise her they would make sure no one ever found out about her mother. But it was a risk she was not willing to take.

"You could try," Albert said softly, his hand reaching up to rest on her arm. "Where he wounded you, I want only to help you heal. Where he crushed you, I want to see you thrive. I will devote every single one of my best intentions to you, and you alone."

"Why?" Rebecca asked.

"Because I love you, Rebecca Bedford."

She turned toward him at the proclamation, her round eyes growing bigger, tears spilling. He had done it. He had forced her hand. Now she would have to hurt him, even if it broke her to do so. He raised a finger under her chin, tilting her head back, and they studied one another.

"Albert," she whispered. "After everything we have learned? Knowing it will be an uphill battle to be with me because of it all?"

"After it all," he nodded. "I love you."

Her eyes closed, and she swallowed hard. "Oh, Albert…"

She heard the tone of her voice, how it betrayed her. For while her mind screamed at her to tell him no, to throw up her walls, close the gate, and begin hurling cannonballs toward any thought of love, she also desperately wanted the man standing in front of her to be with her every day for the rest of her life.

Albert must have heard the desire in her voice, for he drew close. He placed his hands on either side of her face and she stepped nearer to him as he gently tilted her head back. Softly, tenderly he kissed her. It had been so long since she had been kissed, and she was certain John had never kissed her in the way Albert was. There was a connection between them she had never known before, and if she could only never have a realistic and coherent thought again, she was confident they could find every happiness together.

But the flood of thoughts could not be contained

for long. When he pulled back, his hands still cradling her face, his thumb running from the bottom of her lip to her chin, she remembered what a horrible mistake they were making. She would ruin him.

"Trust grows in time," he reminded her. "Could... could you try, Rebecca?"

"I can't," she whispered, running her hand through his hair. "It is not just about trust, Albert. I know you would earn it quickly. You are a good man. Such a good man. But that is why we can never be more than friends. My reputation, and the scandal we have added by uncovering my mother's past, if anyone in my family turns out to have murdered my mother. Albert, it would ruin the Harrington name for you to be tied to me. Think of your brother, your niece. You could never do that to them. You would never forgive yourself."

She had hit a sore spot, made her point. She could tell by the way his grip lightened and his gaze lowered to the floor.

"It would be fine," he argued, though she heard the uncertainty through which he said.

"No, Albert. It wouldn't. I couldn't live with it. Please, let's not torture ourselves this way."

He looked at her, tears brimming his eyes, pleading with her. She saw his mind turning, searching for a solution as if this were a criminal case and not their tangled lives. But at last, he released her, stepping away, and she was overcome with cold. Her arms tightened around herself, and they stared at one another.

"I have to leave," he said quickly, voice breaking.

She nodded, watching as he turned on his heel and walked out of the room without a second glance. She fell to the settee, shocked by what had happened. The last weeks had been too trying, too exhausting, and she had not the strength to go on. She just breathed shallowly, quaking beneath the weight of her mother's portrait staring down at her.

When Henry entered the house sometime later, Rebecca had moved to the piano again and her fingers moved softly, weakly over the keys. Never had she found herself in such a despondent and sorrowful state. It was as if the world continued to spin without her. She had lost all track of time, floating along in what she was sure would be an eternal, pensive gloom.

In a matter of weeks, Albert had become the world to her, and she to him. But it was not to be. She had once laughed at the preposterousness of

Shakespeare's *Romeo and Juliet*. Star-crossed lovers? Fate? It was all a romantic hoax.

Only now, as she heard and felt Beethoven's fourteenth sonata coming from the instrument before her, her theory had been completely thrown off course. She had no control over the love and adoration for Albert Harrington that had rooted and developed in her heart. It had been beyond her command. Her heart had run ahead of her and she had lost herself to him.

"Play something cheerful, sister," Henry's voice interjected into her gloom.

She frowned, head hanging lower. His hand landed on her shoulder.

"Come, you know I dislike that one. Makes me feel melancholic."

Still, she remained silent.

"I've come from an errand that I think will capture your fancy."

Rebecca turned to him at last as he brought a chair near her and sat.

"You inspired me, you know, with your stubborn refusal to give in and marry John, knowing he would make you miserable. You inspired me to go after what I truly want. To put aside opinions of others, and to lay the whole situation out in front of me. View it through my eyes alone. And I came to a conclusion that will please Father. Not that it was my aim to please, but it will, nonetheless. I think it will take some of the pressure off of you to find an advantageous marriage."

"What are you on about, Henry?" she asked, head spinning and impatience bubbling to the surface. She had not the energy for her little brother's excited rambling.

He grinned. "Rebecca, I've been honest about my feelings for someone. Asked permission to court her, and I've received a yes from both her and her father."

Rebecca's heart pounded in her ears. Could she take this announcement? Would it bring about her worst fears? And could she handle losing a brother to marriage when her own heart ached with such loneliness? How could she face this house without him in it? How could she face having a sister-in-law who was so cruel?

She attempted to slow and pace her thoughts. This was courtship, not marriage. He had not told her who just yet. Hope remained.

"Who, Henry?" she asked bravely.

"Anne. Anne Whitlow."

She could not swallow.

"Anne Whitlow," she stated.

"Yes," Henry beamed. "I know you don't always get along, but you can set all that aside. She will be your sister by the end of next year, I am certain. You will learn to adore each other."

Rebecca pounced to her feet. "You cannot be serious."

He stared up at her in surprise, mouth hanging open.

"Henry. She's cruel. She's a gossip."

"She's apologized for all of those things to me."

"But still, she does them!"

"Rebecca, she's truly not as bad as you make her out to be. She's sweet. Give her a chance. Get to know her as I have."

"I've known her since she was seven. I know all I need to know."

"Rebecca," he spoke softly, standing and reaching for her hand. "I promise. You will learn to care for her as a sister, in time."

"Why in the world would I ever do that?"

"Because I love her. She will be my wife. And you must."

His voice was authoritative, challenging, and full of command. He had never spoken to her that way before, and it struck her just how much he sounded like their father. Tears stung at the corner of her eyes and she turned her head away obstinately. He released her hand as if it revolted him and stormed from the room, the door slamming behind him, glass rattling in the frames.

She could take no more. Sobs threatening to erupt from her, she crossed the room to the writing table, pulled out a card and pencil, and scribbled out a note.

*Mr. Albert Harrington,*

*Please delay our course of action until further notice. I will contact you again should I decide to proceed.*

*Miss Rebecca Bedford*

"Edwin!" Rebecca called out, knowing the butler would be nearby as she folded the note.

"Yes, Miss?" He appeared in the doorway.

"Please make sure this gets to the Harrington residence first thing in the morning."

## CHAPTER 10

To say he was devastated did not do justice to Albert's feelings after Rebecca rejected him. He was disappointed in himself for not fighting harder, but after the comment she had made about ruining the Harrington name, a very good point indeed, he could not find a way out. When it had just been the scandal of John Templeton, Albert had not cared in the least. He did not believe Rebecca to be at fault in the situation and believed that with time, the whole thing would be forgotten. In fact, Rebecca marrying him might have even sped that process up.

But this new scandal they had uncovered was much bigger. Impossible, most would say, to recover from. A child out of wedlock? If the truth of that came out, the Bedford name would be ruined. Their money would be worthless. Their social standing would be ripped out from under them. It was no wonder Hannah Bedford and her parents had gone to such great lengths to cover it up. He wondered why she had dared to keep any mementos of the whole event in the house at all. A mother's love, he suspected, was the only reason she had. Hannah had been powerless to forget the child, knowing her daughter lived and was growing up in the world without any idea as to who her mother was.

It had to have been a painful existence Hannah had endured. And there was a painful existence Rebecca endured now, perhaps soon to be made worse. This world they lived in was cruel to anyone who did not fit the desired mold of wealth, respect and grace. Any hint of a blemish in a woman's life would send her toppling into a place of rejection. Coldness, turned backs, and harsh whispers followed Rebecca everywhere she went. He had seen it firsthand, how she was there with them all, but not wanted.

On top of all of that, was the matter still unsolved. Had Hannah been purposefully poisoned? Or had she committed suicide, unable to deal with her mental agony any longer? That alone was enough to bury the family in shame. In this Catholic world their society lived in, it would mean that Hannah or someone in their household had committed an unpardonable sin. That would follow Rebecca around her entire life.

Yes, he had to admit, there did not seem to be any way around the whole thing. And he was not the least bit surprised to receive the note from Rebecca calling off the investigation the following morning. He had known the note would come, knew she would try to cut him out of her life, but he was determined to ignore it. There was not a chance he would walk away. His love for her was too great. Even if he did not love her as he did, he would have continued the investigation until he figured out how Hannah Bedford died. There was the remaining possibility that there was a murderer living somewhere in the Bedford home.

He did love her though, more than anything or anyone else. He was sure that if he and Rebecca could agree to continue hiding it all, they could move on with their lives. Even if it did come out, he could survive as long as he had Rebecca by his side. He wanted her, loved her, that intensely, he could envision himself surviving any scenario as long as he was with her. Even if it meant dissolving his ties to the Harrington name.

The thing that concerned him most was Rebecca's mental state. He knew that if she locked herself away from the world, away from love, she would grow cold and miserable. Albert desperately wanted her to see and believe in the grace and forgiveness he had found in God. His heart had changed forever. He had real hope. He wanted her to have that too, as he was sure it was the only way she could truly find joy.

Albert spent his morning on his knees in prayer. He prayed for wisdom. He prayed for Rebecca's heart. And he prayed for a way out, a peaceful resolution to the situation. He prayed for the desires of his heart to be in line with God's will.

He spent that afternoon chasing his niece around the garden, listening to her squeals and peals of laughter, wondering how he could risk the little girl's future by pursuing Rebecca Bedford. But at the end of the evening, when he finally settled in bed, he felt a calmness wash over him. His Heavenly Father was singing words of comfort and promise over him. And Albert fell asleep knowing that his faith and trust were being grown within his heart. And with the desire to be with Rebecca, to chase after her, rooted more firmly within him, he knew without a doubt that loving her was a calling from the Lord.

Albert had been invited to dinner at the Bedford residence that Sunday, and Rebecca dreaded it with everything in her. The invitation had been sent by her father who was entirely unaware of what had transpired between them.

The butterflies in her stomach that afternoon were intense. The only thing she could do to ease her nerves as the time for him to arrive drew ever closer was to pound away at the piano keys. When she heard the knock at the door, it was all she could do to keep her fingers moving. She heard Henry stand and saw Albert's form in the doorway from the corner of her eye, but she dared not look up at him.

"Hello, Albert," Henry greeted.

"Henry," Albert returned the greeting.

"I'll leave you alone," Henry said. As he passed Albert, he muttered, "Rebecca's in quite the mood. Good luck."

"Albert!" Her father boomed. "Welcome, son. We are glad to have you."

"Thank you, sir. I am happy to be here."

He sounded less than happy, Rebecca noted, and still, she could not bring herself to look at him. She knew she would lose her resolve if she did.

"Henry has gone out to meet Anne's carriage, I believe. We are happy to have her joining us for dinner tonight as well. Aren't we Rebecca?"

Rebecca heard the dare in his voice. Anne's presence had been the topic of great argument all afternoon amongst the three of them. Rebecca had made her opinions very known, much to the chagrin of both Henry and her father. Rebecca hit a sour note purposefully, slamming the cover down over the keys and whirling toward him. She would not hold back, she decided. She would rain her fury down on all of them. She was too exhausted not to.

"Yes," she smirked. "Delighted."

She glanced toward Albert for the first time to find him staring at her in shock. She looked him square in the face. "Henry has decided he is in love with Anne," she explained. "I know she's your cousin, Albert, but she is truly awful."

"Rebecca Elizabeth!" Her father chastised her. "I implore you to hold your tongue."

"She is a bit of a gossip," Albert admitted with a shrug. "And I am sure she has been quite terrible to you, Rebecca. She says what she thinks others want to hear more than she speaks her own mind. But she is sweet when you get to know her."

Rebecca sighed. It seemed everyone was determined to love Anne Whitlow. But they had not overheard the way Anne had talked about her over breakfast that morning she had been out with Henry. She had not been the only one, she knew.

Harriet had been there as well. But there was no excuse.

"We will have dinner soon," her father said, tucking the newspaper away. "Rebecca, go check on the progress of dinner preparations while Albert and I talk business."

She did as she was told. The meal was prepared, they were simply awaiting Anne. Gran had called off with a headache, and Rebecca was thankful she would have the reprieve from that woman's opinions at least. She was crossing back from the dining room to the parlor when Anne and Henry came bounding in on each other's arms, both of them laughing. Rebecca was assaulted by the noise and unexpected intrusion on her journey.

"Oh, Rebecca!" Anne greeted, releasing her hold on Henry and wrapping her arms around Rebecca. "It is so good to see you."

Rebecca remained stiff and did not return the hug. Her voice sounded stiff too. "You as well, Anne."

Anne pulled away, her face sober as she grasped Rebecca's hands in her own. "I should have called on you after the ball, but I was just fit to be tied. I was so embarrassed that my father had invited Mr. Templeton. It took me days to find out why he had done so when it had so clearly upset you, but when I found out your father had requested it, and had invited him back to Victoria well… I was sure I had misunderstood the whole thing. But please tell me, Rebecca… are you hurt? I will do whatever I can to make it up to you."

Rebecca had turned her gaze from Anne toward the parlor the moment she had outed her father. Her gaze landed on the man coming forth from the room, Albert just behind him. Never had she laid such a ruthless glare on her father's form. After everything John had put her through, all the tears and drama, the general disarray that young man had left in this house, her father had invited him back. It was the worst betrayal she had ever known.

She would address it but willed herself to be silent until her guests were gone. She would behave as her mother raised her to for as long as Anne was in this house. And then she would unleash her wrath upon her father.

After she assured Anne of her forgiveness through gritted teeth, they moved to the dining room together. They made it through two courses of the meal, Rebecca quite proud of how she was behaving. If only she could get Albert to stop gazing at her as he was.

It was clear to Albert that something had happened between Anne and Rebecca in the entryway. He had seen the icy look she gave her father. He was glad in that moment he was not the one on the receiving end of it. But as time went on, Albert felt terribly like he was more aware of the unfavorable undercurrent in the room than anyone else was. Each member of the Bedford family kept a close eye on one another, staring each other down during different moments of the evening. Rebecca's every movement was harsh and rigid.

Rebecca sat at his side, Henry and Anne across the table from them, and Paul Bedford at the head of the table. The conversation was pleasant enough. He had not visited with Anne since he had returned from school for more than a passing conversation. She was a bit silly, he would admit, and had little opinions of her own. He recognized a timidity in her, that he figured was heightened by sitting across the table from a woman so opposite her.

Where Anne was shy, Rebecca was bold. Where Anne lacked knowledge and conviction, Rebecca was well-studied and opinionated. And Albert recognized something that Rebecca certainly did not: Anne Whitlow had a fear of Rebecca Bedford borne out of nothing short of reverence. Anne wanted nothing more than for Rebecca to accept her.

Rebecca was polite enough to her, but not warm. He guessed Rebecca was either oblivious of the mutual adoration between Henry and Anne, or she was ignoring it completely.

But Albert was less concerned about what was going on between Anne and Rebecca than he was the distance between the two of them. Sitting there next to her, so hopelessly in love with her, was a challenge. Doing so under the studious gaze of her father was worse.

He tried to distract himself by watching the household staff serve each course of the meal. It did little to help. The most distraction came when Alice stopped to whisper something in Rebecca's ear. As Albert watched them speak quietly with each other, it struck Albert that something seemed incredibly familiar about the lady's maid. He had never given her more than a glance before that moment. But he could not place her with a memory and was soon bored with that line of thought as well.

"Should we go out to the garden?" Rebecca suggested after the final course was served.

"Wait," Henry spoke up. "We have some news I would like to share with you first."

As soon as Albert saw the look that passed

between Anne and Henry and saw the way their hands intertwined on the table, he had little doubt about what was to come. But before another word could be uttered, Rebecca stood quickly to her feet.

"Henry, please," she begged. "Do not do this tonight."

"Rebecca! Sit down!" Paul Bedford roared. "I have had quite enough of you marching around here acting as if you run this house. Your brother has something he wishes to share, and you will listen, and you will be happy for him."

"I won't!" Rebecca exclaimed, tears brimming her eyes. "You cannot make me!"

Albert jumped in surprise at her loud outburst.

"Rebecca…" Henry pleaded.

"No, Henry! Do not do this. Please. I beg you."

Anne looked ready to crawl under the table, her face pale. "I… I do not understand."

"Everything is all right," Henry assured her.

"It is not all right!" Rebecca argued. "I will stand up for myself in this! Anne, you have been cruel to me! You have sought countless opportunities to humiliate me and spread malicious gossip about me. I have heard you with my own ears. You have never been a friend to me. You have cast judgement on me and cast me out. And you want me to call you a sister?"

Anne cowered, shaking and sobbing. "Rebecca… please. I am so sorry."

"I have been miserable. And you have had a part in making me so. I cannot…"

Rebecca fled the room, and Albert felt himself following her before he realized he was doing so. He found her out in the garden, sobbing on a bench. He was shocked by what had just happened, by what had occurred over the course of the entire evening. Never before had he seen her loose such control of her emotions. But he knew that it had been building within her for a long time. He had not been back in Victoria long, and even he knew how awful the other women were toward her.

He felt a strong urge to take her in his arms, and this time he did not fight it. She pushed him away at first and he relented. But soon she was leaning into him anyway, and he felt her give in. She continued to sob, turning her face into his neck, her hand grasping at his shirt. His hand rubbed over her back as she cried, his heart longing to take her pain away. Slowly, she began to calm.

"Hush now," he told her after a while.

"Albert…" she breathed out. "I…"

"You lost control of your temper. It happens to the best of us. It is not the end of the world."

She shuddered. At last, she pulled back, and he

began wiping her tears away with his thumbs. He hated to see her green eyes so full of pain.

"I thought I would feel better. I've wanted to say that to her for so long. But I feel worse."

"When my father died, and I was determined to stay my course to study law, Robert said horrible things to me. Words of hatred. He told me I was no longer his brother. So I left, certain we would never speak again. I did not think he would ever forgive me, and I was not sure I could ever forgive him either."

"But you seem to get along now," Rebecca frowned.

"He was always stronger than I was. He wrote to me, apologized profusely. He told me how betrayed he had felt by me, how lost after father died, and the amount of pressure he felt to make him proud. And I had left him to deal with it alone, so he had been hurt. He had pushed me away."

"You forgave him?"

"No," Albert shook his head, smiling sadly at the memory. "I shoved that letter in my desk and did not read it again for months. I was so caught up in how mistreated and misunderstood I had been. I had read his attempts at explanation as excuses. So, he wrote me again. And on that letter were four simple words. 'Albert, I love you.'"

He turned to Rebecca with tears in his eyes. "I went to church that following day, completely broken. My bitterness had destroyed me. I had been trying to punish Robert for his mistakes, make him miserable, but the truly miserable one was me. I could barely remember at that point what had been said between us, why I was angry, but the anger had consumed me."

Albert gauged her reaction and saw a glimmer of understanding flicker across her face.

"We made peace with each other and healed with time," Albert said simply.

"Albert… I do not …I do not think I can make peace with her. It is far too much to overcome now."

"No, my love, there is nothing too much to overcome."

Rebecca was on her feet. "Please. Don't call me that. We cannot do this. You know we cannot."

He wanted to state his case again, plead with her, but knew he could push her no further.

"I am going to go home," he told her. "Thank you for dinner."

He left her standing there in the garden, tears still streaming down her face, even though it was the hardest thing he felt he had ever done. There were some wounds only Jesus could heal. And he would pray about that all night.

Hours later, he pulled his well-worn Bible from his desk. On small pieces of paper, he normally used to make notes in his law books, he wrote out an explanation of the gospel and placed the notes in various places throughout the gospels and the book of Romans. Satisfied with his work, he wrapped the beloved Bible in brown paper and took it downstairs to have it sent to the Bedford residence at once. If she would not see him right now, he would have to let the notes and the Word speak for him.

## CHAPTER 11

*R*ebecca sat curled up in the window seat of her bedroom the next morning, staring at the Bible on her bed with a look of curiosity and disdain. She had opened the package from Albert, expecting something to do with the investigation. Instead, she found a Bible with his name inscribed at the bottom. Pieces of paper had been sticking out of it, and she had opened to one of them. It directed her to read Romans 3:23, which he had underlined.

*"For all have sinned and come short of the glory of God."*

She had snapped it closed and tossed it on the bed, sure he was scolding her and rubbing salt in an open wound. Then she had resumed her current spot in the window. Thirty minutes passed as her mind cycled the words. The reality rolled over her that Albert had never once scolded her for anything. He had encouraged her to forgive her mother once, but it had not been a scolding. He was not the kind of man who would do so.

Her mind was alight with thoughts. At the end of her rope, with her heart in a thousand pieces, and with shame and pain coursing through her veins, Rebecca needed something she could not name.

Bravely, she crossed back to the bed and reopened the book. She noticed this time that all the notes placed in the book of Romans had numbers in the top corners. They were meant to be read in a certain order. So she followed the simple directions and flipped through them one at a time, reading his notes as she did. *"Hear this one, Rebecca. To receive salvation, we must confess that Jesus is Lord and that he died for our sin. We must believe deep in our soul that Jesus was raised from the dead. Confess and believe. Trust and surrender."*

She read the verse multiple times. She read his note multiple times. But it was not that simple, she was sure. There was more. There had to be. She needed to do more. Be more holy. Surely, she had to do something more than just believe.

Rebecca flipped to the next verse which further confused her. Once again, it was simply laid before her. She needed only to believe. The note on that page told her to flip to another place, Romans 8, and to read the whole chapter. She did so, the first time with a frown on her face and her heart pounding rapidly. The second time, with her finger tracing under the words, trying desperately not to miss a single one. And the third time, she felt as though her heart had stopped as she came to the end. She looked up toward the light streaming in the window.

It was with desperation that she tugged open the attic door, flipped on the light, and trudged bravely up the stairs. The room was a little less frightening now. She knew that was in part because she had been up here with Albert not long ago and she had felt safe then. Nothing terrible had happened. At the same time, her lack of fear came from being so deep in a pit of despair, she would almost welcome whatever frightening thing the attic held.

She returned to the trunk and pried it open. It gave way more easily this time, though the hinges still creaked. This time the grief did not come so strongly. She had hardly anything to give it. The trunk was considerably less organized than last time, and she remembered the way Albert had rushed to tuck it all back in and close it before Alice discovered them.

She loved him so dearly that her heart ached at

the thought of it. It was a pain she had not known when John had hurt her. This pain was different. It made her physically ill. She wished she had never started the investigation and that they could have found their way to one another in time. He would have never known about her mother's love child or the suspiciousness of her death. Rebecca would not have known either. In time, she likely would have put the diaries out of her mind and moved on.

Now she had uncovered a truth she could not bury. It would torment her. She wanted to know what had happened to her mother, but apart from questioning everyone who had been around her mother in those final days, without questioning her father, the answers would likely never come. So how could she reconcile who her parents were to the Heavenly Father she had read about in the Bible? She did not know. She knew God was holy. He was pure and good. Albert's notes in Romans had led her to understand that God was not a God waiting for her to make a mistake so He could punish her. He was a God of grace and love.

Rebecca had not known love since her mother died. Not until Albert had walked back in to her life. Albert and his new understanding of God. But she longed to be loved with everything she was. In a world full of pain, broken promises and betrayal,

Rebecca knew she had reached a place only God could pull her from.

"Father…" she breathed out, unsure of what she was doing, but her voice becoming stronger with every word. "Everything has fallen apart. I wanted answers. I found pain. I do not understand this world around me. It is cruel. It is hard for me to believe that you are not. But I want to. I want to believe."

She took a shaky breath. A verse floated through her mind, followed by Albert's words. *"To receive salvation, we must confess that Jesus is Lord and that he died for our sin. We must believe deep in our soul that Jesus was raised from the dead. Confess and believe. Trust and surrender."*

What else could she do? She wanted to believe. She wanted the assurance Albert talked about. She wanted to be a peacemaker. And she wanted to be loved by her Heavenly Father.

"I confess that I am a sinner," Rebecca began again. "That was apparent last night. I have sinned. I have been selfish and bitter and unforgiving. I ask you to forgive me, Lord. I know I do not deserve it, but the Bible says I do not have to deserve it. You are offering it to me. And I want you to know that I believe. I believe all of those words, even if I am not sure I understand all of them yet. I want to. I… want to love you, God, the way Albert does."

A small glimmer of joy and hope swelled within her, and she found herself smiling. She continued to pray for a long time as thoughts drifted through her mind. As she did so, she sifted through the box of baby things once more, her hand trailing over the blonde lock of hair and cradling the ballet slipper. For the first time, she prayed for the sister she knew was out there somewhere in the world, knowing that God knew exactly where she was. She prayed that her sister would also learn to understand God's love one day soon. When she left the attic, she kept the ballet slipper with her as a reminder of what had transpired in the attic that morning and a reminder to pray for her sister every day.

By midafternoon, Albert was walking toward the Bedford house. He needed to see Rebecca, to talk to her about the Bible he had sent her, to talk about what had happened the night before. He would go whether or not he was welcome. He loved her. And he was determined.

She was at the piano when he entered, playing a tune that was surprisingly joyful, and Albert asked

Edwin not to announce him. He had cut a single rose for her from Caroline's garden, and he held it carefully in his hand. His heart raced as he saw her sitting there unaware of his presence.

He placed the rose on top of the piano, which was littered with sheet music and a ballet slipper. The same slipper that had been in Hannah's attic trunk. Rebecca had apparently gone back to retrieve it, though why, he could not be sure. Then his beloved looked up at him with a beautiful, warm, peaceful smile, and he knew exactly why that slipper was sitting out in the open.

"Rebecca?" he asked softly, hope filling him.

"Oh, Albert," she began, tears coming. "I understand now. What you said at dinner that night about the gospel. I understand. Or at least... I am beginning to."

Albert felt his heart swell and he knelt beside her. "Truly?"

Rebecca nodded. "I've behaved badly. I am sorry, Albert."

"You are forgiven," he told her, kneeling before her and reaching for her hands.

They stared at each other for a moment, both of them grinning. Every bit of the harshness he had last seen was gone from her features. She had begun anew, which he could only hope meant they could as well.

"Well… now what?" he asked.

"Stay for tea?" she offered, which he gladly agreed to. He had no idea where they would go from here, but he was glad he was welcome here again. He settled in to stand near the piano and turn the pages as she played.

"Alice," Rebecca turned to the woman sitting in her usual corner. "Will you ring the bell for a tray of tea, please?"

Alice nodded, setting aside her book and limping toward the door to ring the bell.

"Alice, are you injured?" Albert asked with concern.

"No, sir. Just an old injury from when I danced as a young girl. It bothers me before rainstorms."

Albert nodded and as the woman left the room, he let his eyes drift back to Rebecca as she began to play. He watched, eyes drifting over the sheet music before him. Famous composers, some of which he had heard her play before. His eyes drifted to the portrait of Hannah hanging above the mantle. He studied the woman for a long moment, taking in her features and noting once more how much Rebecca looked like her.

The tea arrived and as Alice set about preparing

it, a crash drew his attention away from the painting. The lady's maid looked up as Albert felt more than saw Rebecca whirl around to see what had happened. His eyes landed on Alice's crimson cheeks, embarrassed and stumbling over apologies about a broken teacup as Rebecca compassionately moved to help clean up the broken china.

Albert gasped softly. As he reflected on the moment later, he was certain he would not have seen it at all if his eyes had not traveled directly from the painting to Alice's face. But there it was, just the same; Hannah Bedford's brown eyes staring back at him, and her nose too. Topped with a head of blonde hair. And then his eyes landed on the ballet slipper.

"Alice," he muttered. "Helena Mary Alice."

"What?" Rebecca asked over her shoulder at him.

"Mary Alice. The child…the ballet slipper…the injury…" he spelled it out, loud enough for Alice to overhear. "The blonde hair. Your mother's eyes."

Rebecca remained crouched on the floor with the broken teacup in her hand, looking at him in confusion as she tried to make sense of what he was saying. And then he pointed at Alice and she looked at the woman who was barely two years older than her. She was on her feet almost immediately, and Albert rushed to her side, unsure what she would do.

"Alice! It's you!" Rebecca exclaimed in realization,

and Alice's wide brown eyes flew up to look at her.

Rebecca was visibly shaking, and Albert placed his hands on her arms.

"Rebecca, hold on. Let's be sure."

"Miss Rebecca?" The woman stuttered, though from her panicked expression and pale face, it was obvious. She was caught.

"You have been here this whole time! How... How did you manage it?" Rebecca demanded.

Rebecca could not believe what was happening. Black spots swam at the corner of her vision. Alice was already tearing up, and Rebecca stared at her in angry disbelief.

"Please, you must understand. My father died when I was twelve. He told me everything before he died, about my mother... about our mother."

Rebecca flinched under the statement.

"He wrote to an old friend, someone who had known about their affair and kept it a secret... someone who had traveled with my mother to France while she still carried me. Someone who had remained with our mother even when she came here to marry Mr. Bedford... her lady's maid, Margaret Smith. They had remained in contact. It was how mother, Mrs. Bedford, received information and trinkets about me. They were all sent through Margaret. He told Margaret he was dying and secured a training position under her here in this house where I could grow up around my mother, my family, without anyone knowing."

"Did my father know about this?" Rebecca asked weakly.

"No, ma'am," Alice shook her head. "Not even Mother knew. Only Margaret. I worked hard to secure my place here, Miss Rebecca. Worked to earn your trust. I've been solely devoted to you, please know that. Please, Miss… you must understand, it was an accident. Truly it was."

"What was?" Albert coerced.

"She found out," Alice whispered. "I will never know how. But she found out. I was helping Margaret more and more in those last days. Her hands were arthritic. And while I worked, Mother— Mrs. Bedford—watched me closely. One day, the day of her death, she asked Margaret to leave the room. She stared at me for a long time, I was shaking so badly… and she told me she knew who I was. Threatened to fire me if I ever dared breathe a word to anyone. Said it would ruin her family. That it would ruin you, Miss Rebecca. I offered to do anything, anything at all. And then she consoled me, told me it was all right, that she had always loved me. That she was glad I was there. I was so baffled, nervous… you have to understand."

"What did you do?" Rebecca demanded, blood pounding in her ears.

"She asked me to give her the medicine, the white powder. Told me how much to give her. I thought I did exactly what she said. I have been over it countless times since, but I gave it to her and then…" Alice dissolved in a puddle of sobs, falling at Rebecca's feet. Her face fell flat against the floor. "I am so sorry. So sorry, Miss Rebecca. I loved her. I did. I did not mean to, you have to know that. It was a mistake."

Rebecca was clearly stunned and frozen in her spot as Alice repeated her apology once more. Albert, however, knelt next to the woman, timidly placing a hand on her shoulder.

"She should have never asked you to give her medicine without a doctor present. You had no training. You could not have known." Albert looked her square in the eyes. "It is a lot to live with, to be sure, but it was not your fault."

Rebecca took a moment to let the truth set in. She took deep breaths, terribly afraid she might pass out. Albert rose to his full height next to her, his arm going around her waist.

"Rebecca?" he asked softly. "Are you all right?"

"I prayed for you," Rebecca responded. "Alice. I prayed for you this morning. I prayed for my sister. Whoever or wherever she was. You were right here the whole time."

"I am so sorry, Miss Rebecca. I wanted to tell you so many times… but I knew you had no idea I existed. I did not think you would believe me."

"We've been investigating," Albert spoke up, his arm squeezing Rebecca closer. "We learned you existed a few days ago."

"I prayed for you," Rebecca repeated, feeling the shock wearing off. She removed herself from Albert's side, needing space, and crossed the room to the piano. She picked up the ballet slipper.

If her mother were here, Rebecca would look her straight in the eyes and tell her everything was going to be all right. That she forgave her for keeping the secret, that she understood. But this woman standing in the room now… her sister… She prayed for the strength she needed to forgive her.

Only hours before, she had asked God to forgive her. Now she stood at a crossroads. Would she extend forgiveness to this woman? She had lied for years. She had betrayed her by holding back her true identity. And though it had been an accident, her mother was dead now because she had given her the wrong dosage of medicine. They had reached the resolution of the whole mystery, and she felt a turmoil in her she had never known. It would take her entire life, she knew, to reconcile herself to the pain her mother must have endured over her life. And yet her mother had remained so kind. So forgiving. So full of grace.

Grace. That was a word Albert had spoken of when he had told her how God was not one of judgement, but of grace. And mercy.

Rebecca felt a new light of realization pass through her heart. She returned to where Alice still sat on the floor in stunned silence, Albert sitting right next to her, but watching Rebecca's every move. Slowly, Rebecca held the ballet slipper out to Alice.

"I believe this is yours?" Rebecca asked softly, her voice full of compassion. Alice's eyes met hers and Rebecca watched her timidly reach up and take the slipper, nodding. Rebecca reached down for her hand and pulled her to her feet.

"I don't want anything from you, Miss Rebecca. I won't tell anyone of this. I'll leave the country if you want… but please…"

Rebecca shook her head. "Alice… I… I will have to find a new position for you in another house. I do not think I could—"

"I understand."

"But I will spend every day of the rest of my life forgiving you. Fighting for that."

Alice flung her arms around her neck, holding her, and Rebecca wrapped her arms around her older sister for the first time.

"We can tell no one. I know," Alice told her.

Rebecca nodded, feeling a bit more at peace. "Take the rest of the day to recompose yourself. I will see you in the morning to discuss what we need to do next. Albert and I will discuss it further."

Alice resumed her normally quiet disposition, bowed her head, and scurried from the room, ballet slipper held close to her heart. Rebecca stared at the empty doorway for a long time and then turned to Albert who was standing several feet away, his face full of empathy as he looked at her.

"Are you—?"

"I am fine," Rebecca told him. "Or… I will be. I am relieved that it is over."

Her eyes drifted to the portrait of her mother hanging over the mantle. "Oh, what she must have endured… to be separated from the man she loved… from her child, by such trivial circumstances as social classes. Albert, I cannot resolve to live that way."

He closed the distance between them. "What do

you mean?"

"I will not lock myself away from the possibility of love, of joy, for something as ridiculous as reputation. I speak so often of wanting to go against their rules and expectations, and yet I've considered giving up everything for them."

She reached for his hands, drawing them up to cradle in her own. She looked straight into his eyes, seeing the faint light of hope sparkling in them and not wanting to ever look away.

"Albert, my darling friend, I love you," Rebecca told him. "I choose to love you, knowing that at any moment, the world we know could change, and I would still have you. If... of course, you will still have me?"

Albert smiled, and she felt and saw all the tension roll out of him. "Oh, Rebecca. Marry me. Marry me, Rebecca Bedford."

Rebecca responded by rising on her tiptoes and kissing him. Her hands released his, sliding instead around his waist as his hands cradled her face gently in his palms. She did not remember ever feeling so loved and wanted before that moment. But gazing into his eyes she knew she would feel that way for the rest of her life, because Albert Harrington would pursue her with all the love, care, and grace he could find.

## NOTE TO READERS

First of all, thank you for taking precious moments of your life to read this book. It has been my dream to have others read my work for my entire life, and I am so thankful you are one of the readers I prayed over while writing. Reviews mean everything to success of authors, so please take one moment more to leave one!

This story took a lot of turns I didn't see coming while I was writing. What began as Rebecca's story, quickly became Albert's. I had so much fun writing these passionate, outspoken, and courageous characters. I loved seeing Rebecca fall in love with Jesus as she fell in love with Albert. I loved seeing her encounter truth, grace and forgiveness. And I admired Albert's courageous faith. My hope is that you encountered the same truths, grace, and love that the characters did.

You can follow me by subscribing on my website, www.audreylaneblenheim.com. I look forward to connecting with you there! Thank you!

## ACKNOWLEDGMENTS

Above all, to my Creator and Savior. I'm falling deeper in love with you every day, and I still can't believe how much you love me. Thank you for giving me this story to write. The words came so quickly there is no way this story is anything but yours.

To Jessica, my editor, and my dear friend. I'm so thankful God brought you into my life and I'm looking forward to working with you on many more projects. (BH Writing Services)

To Molly, Kate, Shauna and Stephanie. You have been there through one of the hardest seasons of my life, speaking truth in grace and reminding me how loved I am. This wouldn't have happened without you.

To Haley, who has been reading my writing since fourth grade, and helping me become a better writer.

To my family at Fellowship Bible Church. Words cannot describe the love I have for you. Thank you for praying over me and encouraging me. Thank you for endlessly striving to be the Church as God designed it to be.

And to Grandma Ann Hoffman. It has been my biggest dream to write a book I could place in your hands. I can't believe that day is here. I love you.

## ABOUT THE AUTHOR

Audrey Lane Blenheim is a twenty-something-year-old disciple of Jesus with a passion for writing Christian fiction. She desires to use this gift to answer God's calling on her life, to share with others the reality of what it means to be "saved by grace."

A rule-follower at heart, Audrey has spent years trying to wrap her head around a God who saves us exactly as we are and where we are, wraps us in forgiveness and grace, and works to refine us daily so that we can look more like Him. Audrey hopes her stories of real struggles, real pain, and real mistakes in people encountering their Savior, will impact the Kingdom and bring glory to the one who saved her soul.

When Audrey isn't writing, she's working in full-time children's ministry in a church in Southwest Missouri, hanging out with a passel of 100 small humans, sipping endless cups of coffee, visiting with friends, and relentlessly cheering on the New Orleans Saints.

Made in the USA
Monee, IL
20 February 2021

60979112R00104